Gilgamesh

Gilgamesh

...

Gilgamesh

The New Translation

Gerald J. Davis

Insignia Publishing

Gilgamesh

ISBN 978-1500256463
(Paperback)

Insignia Publishing
Bridgeport, Connecticut

For Jacob and Teddy

...

Gilgamesh

...

Also by Gerald J. Davis

Beowulf, The New Translation

Don Quixote, The New Translation

Left No Forwarding Address

Jungle of Glass

A Murder Too Personal

...

Gilgamesh

Contents

...

Gilgamesh

...

A Note on the Translation

By

Gerald J. Davis

The *Epic of Gilgamesh* is the oldest story that has come down to us through the ages of history. It predates the *Bible*, the *Iliad* and the *Odyssey*. The *Epic of Gilgamesh* relates the tale of the fifth king of the first dynasty of Uruk (in what is modern day Iraq) who reigned for one hundred and twenty-six years, according to the ancient Sumerian King List. *Gilgamesh* was first inscribed in cuneiform writing on clay tablets by an unknown author during the Sumerian era and has been described as one of the greatest works of literature in the recounting of mankind's unending quest for immortality. Gilgamesh the King is thought to have lived in the period from 2850 B.C. to 2700 B.C., and was later worshipped as a cult hero. The earliest Gilgamesh poems, related in oral form, are believed to have originated around 2200 B.C., and the first in written form around 2000 B.C.

Ancient Sumer was, in all probability, the first civilization in history, established during the fifth millennium B.C. It was the first society to have a written language, which began, according to the latest scholarship, around 3500 B.C. The Sumerians were a non-Semitic people whose likely origins were in northern Mesopotamia. Sumerian was a language with no known analogs; that is to say, it had no relationship to any known existing languages.

Akkadian gradually began to replace Sumerian as a spoken language during the second millennium B.C., but Sumerian continued to be used for religious, legal, ceremonial, scholarly and scientific purposes until about 1800 B.C. The Akkadians were a Semitic people from the West who conquered Sumer about 2300 B.C. Akkadian was the earliest Semitic language, related to Arabic and Hebrew, and the Akkadians, after their conquest of Sumer, adopted cuneiform, which was originally used to write Sumerian.

The clay tablets like those upon which the *Epic of Gilgamesh* were inscribed were in common use in the ancient Middle East. They were generally of a size (about 6" by 7") which could be held easily in one hand and were usually written on both sides. These tablets were inexpensive, easily transported and, when fired, were long-lasting. In the ancient society of Sumer, writing began as a form of record-keeping, and the earliest examples of inventories, accounting records, legal documents and correspondence appear in these clay tablets. The clay tablets, when wet and soft, were impressed with a reed stylus in order to inscribe the wedge-shaped cuneiform characters and symbols. In fact, the word cuneiform is derived from the Latin, *cuneus,* meaning "wedge" and *forma,* meaning "shape."

The meaning and import of these clay tablets was unknown for thousands of years until, in the early nineteenth century, the cuneiform characters began to be deciphered by European scholars. But it was the visit during the 1830s by Major General Sir Henry Rawlinson (1810-1895), sometimes called the Father of Assyriology, a British East India Company Army officer, to Kermanshah in western Persia, which led to the first important breakthrough in the decipherment of these ancient languages. There, carved upon a stone cliff-side on Mount Behistun, is an inscription fifteen meters high by twenty-five meters wide, depicting events that occurred before and during the reign of Darius the Great from 522 B.C. to 486 B.C. This Behistun Inscription is a tri-lingual cuneiform monument written in Akkadian, Elamite and Old Persian. Thus, it is comparable to the Rosetta Stone in that it enabled scholars to decipher a previously undecipherable ancient script. (Unfortunately, this timeless monument suffered damage during World War II when Allied soldiers used it for target practice.) While engaging in combat during the First Afghan War between Britain and Afghanistan from 1839 to 1842, for which he was awarded the Companion of the Order of the Bath for valor in 1844, Rawlinson transcribed and deciphered the inscriptions on Mount Behistun. He presented his results to the Royal Asiatic Society in London and, for his efforts, Rawlinson was elected a Fellow of the Royal Society in 1850 as "The Discoverer of the Key to the Ancient Persian, Babylonian and Assyrian Inscriptions in the Cuneiform Character."

At about the same time, in 1851, an English archaeologist named Sir Austen Henry Layard (1817-1894) unearthed the ruins of the ancient Library of Ashurbanipal in northern Mesopotamia (present-day Iraq). Ashurbanipal was the last major Assyrian king of the seventh century B.C., known as a successful military commander and a renowned scholar. The Library of Ashurbanipal was found to contain tens of thousands of clay tablets and fragments, among them the *Epic of Gilgamesh.* Most of these tablets and fragments were subsequently transported to England and can be viewed as part of the collection of Assyrian antiquities in the British Museum, of which Layard was appointed a Trustee in 1866.

But the true hero of the *Epic of Gilgamesh* is an Englishman named George Smith (1840-1876). Poor and of humble background, Smith left school at the age of fourteen and became the apprentice to a printer. He married young and eventually had six children. However, bored by his work and entranced by ancient history, he began to frequent that collection of Assyrian antiquities at the British Museum in London, not far from his place of employment. Smith spent so much time poring over the cuneiform tablets that he became adept at reading the inscriptions, and he was called to the attention of Sir Henry Rawlinson, who convinced the British Museum to hire Smith at a minimal salary to work on the tablets in its collection and study the cuneiform texts. Smith's work proved so important to the British Museum that he was promoted to the position of Senior Assistant in the Department of Assyriology in 1870. During the course of Smith's study of the tablets, he happened to encounter a fragment of Layard's *Gilgamesh* and its relating of the story of the Great Deluge, together with a description of a Noah-like character, the manner of construction of the ark, the embarkation of the animals, the birds sent forth to seek dry land and the ark coming to rest upon a mountain. (This segment is from Tablet XI of the Epic.) When Smith deciphered this, in 1872, he said, "I am the first man to read that after more than two thousand years of oblivion." In that year, Smith achieved worldwide renown by his translation and publication of this account of the Great Deluge, and, on December 3, 1872, he presented his paper before the Society of Biblical Archaeology, with Prime Minister William Gladstone in attendance. Smith's discovery was hailed as one of the most important in the history of archaeology and created an overnight sensation in Victorian England, and the news of it was swiftly reported in publications on both sides of the Atlantic. Biblical scholars were stunned to learn of an account of the Great Deluge that may have predated the *Bible* by thousands of years and it upended centuries of scriptural scholarship. Some experts even began to promulgate the theory that the Israelites may have appropriated the story of the Great Deluge for their Hebrew *Bible* during their exile in Babylon in the sixth century B.C.

The Daily Telegraph in 1872 reported Smith's discovery with these words: "IN THE BEGINNING.

History was jealous of Romance until last week; but then suddenly she gave to the world, by the marvelous skill of a scholar in the British Museum, a fragmentary story far more wonderful and entertaining than any work of fiction. Everybody of intelligence has by this time read that narrative which Mr. George Smith has deciphered from the tablets of Ashurbanipal. With what a magic spell those strange broken sentences carried our minds backward! How far backward? Nobody can safely answer that question within ten centuries or so; but very cautious people among the learned speak of six, seven, or even eight thousand years."

There ensued a great public clamor to unearth further parts of the *Epic of Gilgamesh,* and so, in 1873, *The Daily Telegraph* donated £1,000 to the British Museum to fund an expedition for Smith to travel to Nineveh in order to conduct excavations in the hope of finding additional tablets or fragments. Smith had never travelled before, except to Paris, and he found the journey a difficult one. He suffered from both seasickness and homesickness, and he wrote many letters home (with drawings for his children) attesting to his unhappiness at being separated from his family, but also describing his excitement over the discoveries he was making. Smith excavated some important cuneiform tablets during his dig, including a fragment from the missing part of the Flood story. However, warfare between enemy Arab sects was ravaging the area, and *The Telegraph*, in order to save money, wanted Smith to return home, much against his wishes.

Smith returned to London in 1873 to great acclaim. Named "The Distinguished Assyriologue" by the newspapers, Smith received many requests for speaking engagements. *The Telegraph* ran articles with the headline:
"*The Daily Telegraph* Assyrian Expedition Complete
Success of Excavations
The Missing Portion of the Deluge Tablet Discovered."

But Smith was determined to return to Nineveh to continue his excavations. He managed to convince the Trustees of the British Museum to provide £1,000 in order to fund a further expedition and, toward the end of 1873, Smith set out once again. The following year, he unearthed Babylonian accounts of Genesis, containing a description of the Creation, the Fall of Man, the Tower of Babel and other tales, and he related these finds in his book *Assyrian Discoveries* which was published in London in 1875.

The British Museum proposed a third expedition and, after many delays occasioned by local Arab unrest and Ottoman officials (who then ruled Iraq), George Smith arrived in Nineveh in July 1876. By that time of the year it was too hot to dig and a cholera epidemic was spreading throughout the land. Smith's archaeological efforts on this third trip produced meager results. Worried about the widespread deaths from the plague and the difficulties in further digging, Smith wished to return home to his beloved wife and children, whom he missed terribly. He wrote to the British Museum informing them of his intention to journey back to England, and received a stern rebuke in reply. "This the Trustees consider to be very objectionable," wrote the Secretary of the British Museum. The class structure of British society was clearly defined in that era, and Smith was a mere employee of the Museum and a member of the lower orders, who was not afforded the consideration that would have been granted to, say, Sir Henry Rawlinson or Sir Austen Henry Layard.

George Smith, disobeying the Trustees of the British Museum, finally set out for England, but fell ill with dysentery and became delirious before he reached Aleppo, Syria. He died there on August 19, 1876, at the age of thirty-six. In recognition of his accomplishments, Queen Victoria subsequently granted Smith's widow and children a stipend of £150 a year.

This translation of the *Epic of Gilgamesh* is an amalgam of the Sumerian and Akkadian versions, chiefly relying upon the works of Albert T. Clay, Morris Jastrow Jr. and R. Campbell Thompson, supplemented by later excavations and scholarship. The lacunae are filled in using the best judgment of the translator and more recent interpretations based upon the latest findings, for tablets and fragments are still being found up to the present day. However, some priceless tablets were stolen or went missing during the Iraq wars of the late twentieth and early twenty-first centuries.

Many scholars of the ancient Middle East feel that Tablet XII is not properly a part of the *Epic of Gilgamesh*, but rather an Akkadian translation of an earlier Sumerian poem, *Gilgamesh, Enkidu and the Netherworld*. Some view it as an epilogue, reprising the themes of the original Epic, while others view it as an appendage written by an inferior author and thus not worthy of inclusion in the work. For this reason, Tablet XII is listed as Appendix 1.

The Death of Gilgamesh is an earlier Sumerian poem, and does not appear in the Akkadian version of the Epic. It is presented in this book as Appendix 2.

Concerning the matter of the temple harlots, or, as the practice is sometimes called, "sacred prostitution," this custom was common in the ancient world as an integral part of their religious rites. In addition, it is said that the kings of Sumer, as part of the worship ceremony, would engage in sexual intercourse with the high priestess of the Goddess Ishtar in the temple of Eanna in Uruk every year on the tenth day of the New Year festival. As a matter of fact, Herodotus, the fifth century B.C. Greek historian, describes the practice of sacred prostitution in some detail.

There are no footnotes or endnotes in this translation. If any explanations or clarifications are required, they are embedded in the body of the text, so as not to interrupt the flow of the words. After all, as Noel Coward once famously remarked, "Having to read a footnote resembles having to go downstairs to answer the door while in the midst of making love."

Every translation is an interpretation and a series of acts of selection, judgment and calculation. Any mistakes or faults in this edition are solely those of the translator.

And so, herewith, is one of the oldest and greatest works of literature that has come down to us through the dim mists of antiquity.

Black Rock
2014

Gilgamesh

...

Gilgamesh

Tablet I

He had seen all. He all knowledge possessed. Wise was he beyond measure. Gilgamesh was the possessor of all understanding. He had wisdom of all things. He knew of the Secret and of the Mystery. He knew of the time before the Great Flood.

Afar he journeyed and returned home, weary and worn. Whereupon did he grave upon a tablet of stone the account of his travels and his travails. The mighty ramparts of the high-wall'd city of Uruk did he build, and also the walls of the hallowed Temple Eanna, that sacred sanctuary.

Observe well that mighty rampart which shines like unto copper. Behold the lower wall, which the works of none other may equal. Approach the threshold stone, ancient beyond remembrance. Draw near unto that Temple Eanna, dwelling-place of Goddess Ishtar. No King will ever surpass its like.

Ascend the wall of Uruk and upon it walk. Examine the foundations, gaze upon the masonry. Were not the bricks fired in an oven and exceeding good? Did not the Seven Sages lay down its foundations?

The length of one league is the city, one league is the date-grove, one league is the clay-pit, half a league is the Temple of Ishtar. Three leagues and a half is the measure of Uruk.

Seek out the tablet-box of copper. The clasp of bronze unlock. Open the lid and reveal the Unknown. Take up the tablet of lapis lazuli and recite aloud how Gilgamesh underwent all manner of hardship.

Surpassing all Kings, renowned for his stature, Gilgamesh towered over all others. He was the hero, valorous son of Uruk. The great wild bull was he. He took the vanguard in war, as a leader should. The rear guard of his army did he likewise defend. A powerful force was he, protector of his warriors. He was a raging flood-wave, vanquishing even walls of stone.

Gilgamesh was the son of King Lugalbanda and suckling child of the Great Wild Cow Goddess, Ninsun. Gilgamesh was unsurpassed in strength. Taller than all others, he was majestic and fearsome. Mountain passes did he open, and wells did he dig upon the slopes of the mountains.

The oceans did he traverse, and sail the wide seas unto the sunrise, seeking eternal life. Through the force of his invincible might did he journey over a far distance to reach Utanapishtim, the Immortal One, who had survived the Great Flood. Gilgamesh restored the sanctuaries the Deluge had destroyed and brought back the sacred rites for the multitudes.

Which King is the equal of Gilgamesh in magnificence? None can proclaim, as Gilgamesh did, "I alone am King." From the day of his birth there was none other like unto Gilgamesh. Two-thirds of him was a God, one-third of him was a Man. The Great Goddess Aruru, Mother of All Birth, designed the form of his body. Ea, the God of Wisdom, endowed him with perfection. He was perfect in face, perfect in form, perfect in mind.

Gilgamesh was stately in features and lofty in height. Three cubits in length was his foot. The length of half a rod was his leg. His stride was nine cubits. Like unto a God was the beard upon his cheeks. The locks of hair upon his head grew as bountiful as a field of grain. His countenance was well favored and, withal, most comely was he.

Through the city of Uruk did Gilgamesh stride, his head held high, like unto a wild bull, lording it over the people. There was none who could withstand his power. Merciless was he unto the young men of Uruk. He did take the son from his father. The young men of Uruk received ill treatment at his hands. His arrogance swelled with each day and each night.

And the people in their anguish cried out, "Is he our shepherd? Is Gilgamesh the shepherd of the dwellers in Uruk? He, who should be wise, noble and merciful, is instead cruel and heartless. He oppresses the people with great bitterness and with great sorrows."

Gilgamesh left no maiden to her mother, no girl to her betrothed, no bride to her husband. Every maiden did he know. He did lust after all the maidens. His lust was unbounded.

And the people raised their voices in a great lamentation unto the Gods. And it came to pass that the Gods heeded their cries. Whereupon, the Gods of Heaven called out unto Anu, Lord of the Gods, and said, "Did you not breed this mighty wild bull of Uruk? None can withstand his power. He harries the youths of the city with unrelenting cruelty. Gilgamesh leaves no son to his father. By day and by night his tyranny grows unchecked. Is he the shepherd of the people of Uruk? Is he the protector of the people of Uruk? Wise, noble and merciful should he be, but instead he is cruel and heartless. Gilgamesh leaves no maiden to her mother, no girl to her betrothed, no bride to her husband."

Anu, Lord of the Gods, gave ear to their plaints and commanded them to summon Aruru, Goddess of Birth. Unto the Gods did Anu speak thus, "Aruru, it was she who created mankind so numerous. Let her now create one who is the equal unto Gilgamesh. Let her create one who is great in strength, and let him contend with Gilgamesh, that Uruk may have surcease."

And the Gods summoned Aruru, Goddess of Birth, and said unto her, "You, Aruru, did create the multitudes of mankind. Now accomplish what Anu has commanded. Let this creature be the equal of Gilgamesh. His heart make as tempestuous as the heart of Gilgamesh. Let them contend, one with the other, that Uruk may have surcease."

These words did the Goddess Aruru hear. Whereupon she did conceive in her mind what Anu had ordered. Aruru then did lave her hands, did gather some clay and, into the wilderness, did hurl it. In the wilderness did she create valiant Enkidu. Begotten in silence, he was as brave as Ninurta, God of War. Hair covered the whole of Enkidu's body. The hair upon his head was long, like that of a woman. Luxuriant and full, it flowed in the wind like the hair upon the head of Nisaba, Goddess of Grain. Naked was Enkidu, like Sumuqan, God of Animals.

Enkidu knew not people or homestead. On grass did he graze with the wild beasts. He quenched his thirst at water-holes with the wild beasts. Drank he his fill and his heart took delight in the water.

Then, one day, did a hunter chance to come face to face with Enkidu at the water-hole. The hunter beheld Enkidu upon the second day and upon the third day. Whereupon, each time he espied Enkidu, the hunter was struck with terror. He was dismayed and affrighted. There was distress in his breast and woe in his entrails. His face was altered, as one who has travelled upon a wearisome journey.

And the hunter spoke unto his father, saying, "My father, there at the water-hole have I beheld a wild man come forth from the hills. His strength is the greatest in all the length and breadth of this land. Mighty is his power. Like unto a rock fallen from the Heavens is his might. O'er the mountains does he roam all the day. He does graze upon grass with the wild beasts. He quenches his thirst at the water-hole with the wild beasts. I am afeared and dare not approach him. The pits which I hollowed out with mine own hands has he filled in. And the traps which I have set has he torn asunder. He has freed from my clutches the animals that I catch. He will not allow me to do my work."

His father spoke thus unto the hunter, "My son, in Uruk dwells Gilgamesh, the Unvanquished. His strength is the greatest in all the length and breadth of this land. Mighty is his power. Like unto a rock fallen from the Heavens is his might. Go now. Set your face toward Uruk. Seek out Gilgamesh. Unto him relate the might and mischief of this wild man. When he hears of this, he will bestow upon you Shamhat, a harlot from the Temple of Ishtar. Take this temple priestess with you unto the wild man. Over the power of this wild man will she prevail. When next this wild man does draw near unto the water-hole, she shall remove her garment and reveal her beauty. Then shall the wild man espy her and embrace her, and thenceforth shall the wild beasts deny him."

And thus the hunter did hearken unto the counsel of his father and did forthwith set his face toward Uruk to seek Gilgamesh. He spoke these words unto Gilgamesh, the King:

"There is a mighty wild man come forth from out of the mountains. His strength is the greatest in all the length and breadth of this land. Mighty is his power. Like unto a rock fallen from the Heavens is his might. O'er the mountains does he roam all the day. He does graze upon grass with the wild beasts. He quenches his thirst at the water-hole with the wild beasts. I am afeared and dare not approach him. The pits which I hollowed out with mine own hands has he filled in. And the traps which I have set has he torn asunder. He has freed from my clutches the animals that I catch. He will not allow me to do my work."

Unto the hunter did Gilgamesh make reply thus, "Go, hunter, and carry with you, unto the water-hole, Shamhat, a priestess from the Temple of Ishtar. When next this wild man does draw near unto the water-hole, she shall remove her garment and reveal her beauty. Then shall the wild man espy her and embrace her, and thenceforth shall the wild beasts deny him."

And so forth went the hunter, carrying Shamhat the temple harlot with him. Upon their journey did they set out. After the space of three days they arrived at the water-hole. Then did they sit and wait, the hunter and the harlot. One day they waited and a second day they waited, sitting by the place where the wild beasts drank the water. On the third day, the herd of wild beasts came to drink the water. Thither did the animals come that their hearts might delight in the water. And there also was Enkidu, whom the mountains had engendered. He grazed on grass with the gazelles. He slaked his thirst at the water-hole with the wild beasts. Along with the animals did his heart delight in the water.

Shamhat the temple harlot beheld Enkidu, the savage man, begotten in the depths of the wilderness. Then did the hunter speak thus unto her, " 'Tis he, harlot. Uncover your breasts and expose your loins. Let him gaze upon your comeliness. Be not ashamed. When he perceives you, he shall approach you. Remove your garment so he may embrace you. Give him to know the wiles of a woman. Take his seed. Then will the beasts of the wild deny him, since, to his bosom, has he held you."

Then did Shamhat undo her garment and reveal her breasts and her loins. Enkidu saw her nakedness. She felt no shame. Whereupon did Enkidu lie with her and go into her. She gave him to know the wiles of a woman. For the space of seven days and seven nights did Enkidu lie with the temple priestess, his member hard. Then, on the seventh day, was Enkidu's lust sated. He turned his face toward his animals, but they knew him not. The gazelles fled from him when they did behold him. From his presence did the wild beasts flee.

No longer pure was Enkidu. His strength failed him. His legs would serve him not, as he tried to follow after the wild beasts. He was no longer swift. But, withal, Enkidu now had wisdom and enlightenment.

Whereupon, Enkidu sat at the feet of the temple harlot. He turned his eyes to gaze upon her. He listened to the words she uttered. Shamhat the temple harlot spoke thus unto Enkidu, "Wise have you become, Enkidu, like unto a God. No longer need you roam o'er the wilderness with the beasts of the field. Come, I shall carry you unto the high ramparts of Uruk, unto the Temple Sacred, the dwelling-place of Anu and of Ishtar. There lives King Gilgamesh, who is all-powerful and, like a wild bull, he does prevail over all the populace."

Even as she spoke did her words find favor with him. He understood now that he had need of a friend. Then did Enkidu say unto the temple harlot, "Come, Shamhat. Carry me unto the Temple Sacred, the dwelling-place of Anu and of Ishtar. Carry me unto the place where King Gilgamesh lives, he who is all-powerful and, like a wild bull, does prevail over all the populace. I will challenge him, for my strength is great. In Uruk, boldly will I cry aloud, 'I alone am mighty.' There shall I alter destiny. He who was begotten in the wilderness is the possessor of the greatest strength."

And then did Shamhat say unto Enkidu, "Let us journey forth then, that Gilgamesh may perceive your face. Unto Gilgamesh shall I carry you. His dwelling place I know well. We shall journey unto the high-wall'd city of Uruk, where the people are resplendent in their festive attire. Each day in Uruk is a revel. Each day the lyre and the drum do sound. There do the temple harlots, most comely in countenance, entice great men into their beds. O Enkidu, you who are yet so innocent of life, I shall have you know Gilgamesh, the man of many moods. Behold him, regard his face. Observe how mighty is his manhood. His vigor is unsurpassed. He sleeps not, neither by day nor by night. His strength is greater than yours. Therefore, O Enkidu, temper your arrogance. Upon Gilgamesh has Shamash, the Sun God, bestowed his love. Anu, Lord of the Gods, has augmented his knowledge and, likewise, have Enlil, God of Storms, and Ea, God of Wisdom, given him profound understanding. Forsooth, even ere you descended from the mountains had Gilgamesh in Uruk foreseen you in his dreams."

And it came to pass that Gilgamesh arose from his slumber and went to seek his mother, Ninsun, the Great Wild Cow Goddess, to relate his dream unto her. He spoke thus unto her, "O mother, this is the vision I beheld in my dream. Many stars were there in the Firmament. Like unto a rock from the Heavens did one star fall before me. I tried to lift it, but could not. I tried to move it, but could not. The people of Uruk gathered about the rock. The multitudes thronged to behold it. The crowds assembled about the rock and, like unto a suckling babe, did they kiss its feet. Like unto a friend, did I embrace it. Before you did I place it and you, my mother, did account it as mine own equal."

Then did the mother of Gilgamesh, Ninsun, all-knowing and wise, make reply unto her son. Ninsun, the Great Wild Cow Goddess, who understood all, spoke thus unto Gilgamesh, "My son, the stars in the Firmament appeared above you in your dream. Like unto a rock from the Heavens did one star fall before you. You tried to lift it, but could not. You tried to move it, but could not. Like unto a friend did you embrace it. Before me did you place it, and I did account it as your own equal. This is a portent. It augers that a comrade will come unto you, a stout-hearted man will come unto you and stand by you. He shall be your savior. His strength is the greatest in all the length and breadth of this land. Unto your breast like a friend shall you hold him. Mighty is his power. And you shall he save manifold times. This is the meaning of your dream."

And it came to pass that Gilgamesh had a second dream. Whereupon did he approach the Goddess Ninsun, his mother, and say unto her, "Mother, another dream have I had. Upon a street in high-wall'd Uruk did fall from the Heavens an axe. The people of Uruk gathered about the axe. The multitudes thronged to behold it. The crowds assembled about the axe. Like unto a friend, I embraced it. Before you did I place it and you, my mother, did account it as mine own equal."

Then did the mother of Gilgamesh, Ninsun, all-knowing and wise, make reply unto her son. Ninsun, the Great Wild Cow Goddess, who understood all, spoke thus unto Gilgamesh, "My son, that axe which you beheld will be as a companion unto you. Like unto a friend shall you hold him. I shall account him as your own equal. Unto you will come a mighty comrade. He shall be your savior. Great is his power. His strength is the greatest in all the length and breadth of this land. Like unto a rock fallen from the Heavens is his might."

And Gilgamesh spoke unto his mother, saying, "Let this befall according to the command of the Great God, Enlil. May I have a friend to counsel me. A companion shall I have to advise me. This is the meaning of my dream."

Those were the dreams of Gilgamesh.

Whereupon Shamhat, the temple harlot, did relate the dreams of Gilgamesh unto Enkidu, who felt, in his breast, the love of Gilgamesh.

Tablet II

Enkidu sat before Shamhat. The temple harlot uncovered her bosom. Whereupon did Enkidu forget the wilderness wherein he was begotten. So, for the space of seven days and seven nights, did Enkidu lie once again with the priestess and go into her, his member hard. And then did Shamhat the temple harlot speak thus unto Enkidu, "When I behold you, O Enkidu, you are like unto a God. Why is it you wish to roam o'er the wilderness with the wild beasts? Come, let me carry you unto high-wall'd Uruk, unto the Temple Sacred, dwelling-place of Anu. Arise, O Enkidu. I shall lead you unto the Temple Eanna, dwelling-place of Anu and of Ishtar. That is the abode of Gilgamesh, the all-powerful. Him shall you embrace and him shall you love, as you love yourself. Arise from the ground, Enkidu. Arise from the bed of shepherds."

And Enkidu heard her words and approved them as good. The counsel of the woman found favor in his heart. Whereupon, Shamhat did apportion her raiment, so that she might clothe Enkidu therewith. She dressed herself with one part thereof, and did clothe Enkidu with the other part thereof. Then did the temple harlot take him by the hand and lead him like a child unto the huts of some shepherds, unto the place of the sheepfolds.

And the shepherds gathered about Enkidu. The shepherds marveled at the sight of Enkidu. "How like unto Gilgamesh is this man," they did affirm. "He is tall in stature and strong as a battlement. Surely was he begotten in the mountains. His strength is as mighty as a rock fallen from the Heavens."

Before Enkidu did the shepherds set food. They set bread before him, and wine did they set before him. But Enkidu did not eat nor drink, for he knew not these things. Hitherto had he grazed on grass with the wild beasts and sucked the milk of the wild cattle. Enkidu stared at the bread; he stared at the wine. He knew not how to eat the bread. He knew not how to drink the wine.

Then Shamhat, the temple harlot, spoke thus unto Enkidu, "Enkidu, taste of the bread, for it is the staff of life. Drink of the wine, for it is the custom of the land."

And Enkidu ate of the bread until he was sated. He drank of the wine, seven goblets full did he quaff, until his spirits exulted. Glad was his heart and cheerful was his countenance. Then did Enkidu groom his hair and anoint himself with oil. Thus did Enkidu become as a man.

And it came to pass that Enkidu donned a garment and grasped a weapon and was like unto a warrior. Whereupon did Enkidu take up his weapon to do battle with the wolves and the lions who harried the shepherds whilst they did sleep. The wolves did Enkidu rout and the lions did he drive off. Then could the shepherds lie down in peace. They could slumber undisturbed, for Enkidu was their watchman, he who remained awake in the night.

And it befell that, one day, Enkidu did lift up his eyes and espy a man passing by. Whereupon did Enkidu cry out to Shamhat, the temple harlot, thus, "Woman, fetch that man hither. Why has he come? I would know his intention."

The temple harlot called out unto the man and uttered these words, "O Sir, to which place do you hasten in this manner on your arduous journey?"

The traveler drew near and addressed Enkidu thus, "To a wedding banquet do I hie myself. This is the custom of the people. The ceremonial platter shall I heap with plentiful tasty viands for the celebration. Then, after the festivities, for Gilgamesh, King of high-wall'd Uruk, is parted the veil of the virgin bride. Unto Gilgamesh is the chaste girl first offered. The King shall know the wife before her husband. Gilgamesh will be first to lie with the bride. This is ordained by divine decree. From the moment the birth-cord of Gilgamesh was cut, this was destined for him."

Upon hearing these words of the traveler, Enkidu's face grew pale with wrath. And thus did Enkidu speak, "I shall travel unto high-wall'd Uruk, unto the place where Gilgamesh, the King, does rule over the people. And there will I challenge him boldly. There shall I cry aloud in Uruk, 'I am the mightiest in the land. Look upon me and despair.' "

And it came to pass that the twain journeyed unto Uruk; Enkidu walked in front and the woman, Shamhat the temple harlot, walked behind him. They did enter into the great market-place of the city. Whereupon, the multitudes thronged about Enkidu as he stopped in the street. Of Enkidu they exclaimed, "How like unto Gilgamesh is he. Though shorter in height, he is more stalwart in appearance. He is the one who was begotten in the wilderness, who once suckled on the milk of wild beasts and ate of the grass of the forest. Now, at last, for mighty Gilgamesh, like unto a God, has come an equal."

In Uruk was the bridal bed made ready, fit for the Goddess of Weddings. And then were there celebrations and merry-making, and sacrifices offered unto the Gods. Whereupon did Gilgamesh come to the nuptial house to delight in the virgin bride, to go in unto her. But this was not to be, for Enkidu did step forward in the gate and did block the passage of Gilgamesh. Enkidu would permit not Gilgamesh to enter therein.

Then did Gilgamesh and Enkidu grapple, one against the other. Their anger was inflamed, and it burgeoned. Neither one would yield. Like wild bulls did they rage and snort. The stone walls did tremble. The doorposts did shatter. In fierce combat did they struggle, one against the other. The stone walls did tremble. The doorposts did shatter. And then did Gilgamesh overcome Enkidu and place his knee upon the fallen wild man. Thus was Enkidu vanquished.

Whereupon was the fury of Gilgamesh abated. The wrath of the King of Uruk was quelled. And then spoke Enkidu to Gilgamesh, in this manner, "There is none other like unto you. Indeed, the mother who bore you, the Great Wild Cow Goddess Ninsun, exalted you above all other heroes. And the Great God Enlil has destined for you Kingship o'er the people, for none can withstand your might."

And it came to pass that they embraced like brothers and were as friends.

***

And it befell that Gilgamesh would have his mother know Enkidu. So, unto his mother, Ninsun, the Wild Cow Goddess, Gilgamesh spoke thus, "Enkidu is mighty in the land. Great strength he possesses. Like unto a rock fallen from the Heavens is his might. He is tall in stature. Mighty as a battlement is he."

The mother of Gilgamesh made ready to speak. Ninsun, the Wild Cow Goddess spoke unto Gilgamesh in this manner, "My son, in single combat did you fight with Enkidu and overcome him. That was a mighty struggle. You vanquished him in the gate. The stone walls did tremble. The doorposts did shatter. Enkidu has not father or mother. No brother has he. His hair is long and unkempt. In the wilderness was he born. By the wild beasts was he reared. No one has he."

Enkidu stood there. Her words reached his ears. Enkidu grieved at her words. He sat and wept. Tears filled his eyes. His arms lost their power and his strength did desert him. Enkidu breathed a heartfelt sigh. Whereupon did Gilgamesh take the hand of Enkidu and clasp it like that of a brother.

And, upon doing so, Gilgamesh said unto Enkidu, "Wherefore, my friend, do your eyes fill with tears? And why sigh you so mournfully?"

Enkidu made reply unto Gilgamesh thus, "My friend, my strength has deserted me. My arms do fall limp. A cry of sorrow has lodged in my throat. Heartsick am I."

And it befell that Gilgamesh uttered these words unto Enkidu, "Then shall we journey unto the Forest of Cedars, unto the lair of Humbaba, the fearsome giant, Guardian of the Forest, and there shall we slay him, so his Evil will be no more. We shall defeat and destroy Humbaba and drive Evil forth from the land. Then will I cut down the Great Cedar Tree and then shall our names be remembered for all time."

Enkidu spoke these words unto Gilgamesh, "That is why my strength has deserted me and my arms do fall limp. That is why I am heartsick. I am afeared of approaching Humbaba. Know you then, my friend, that, when I roamed the wilderness with the wild beasts, I had knowledge of the Forest of Cedars and of the monstrous giant who dwelled therein. The length of the Forest is ten thousand leagues and the breadth of the Forest is ten thousand leagues. Who would dare venture into the Forest? The Great God Enlil has appointed Humbaba to guard the Forest of Cedars and to strike terror into the hearts of men. Humbaba's roar is like unto the Great Deluge. From out of his mouth spew forth flames of fire and his breath is Death. He hears every rustle of grass in the Forest, though it be a thousand leagues distant. Why desire you to accomplish this deed? Whosoever would dare venture into the Forest of Cedars will find his strength diminished. Weakness will come over him. To struggle against Humbaba is an unequal contest which will end in failure."

Gilgamesh spoke these words unto Enkidu, "My friend, I must climb the mountain and fell the Great Cedar Tree. The tree must be great enough to create a whirlwind as it falls. Then will I be remembered forever. Where is the mere mortal who can ascend to Heaven? It is given only unto the Gods to dwell forever with Shamash, the Sun God. As for men, their life-days are numbered and all their exertions are but like the Wind. Why are you afeared? What of your great strength? Can it be that you dread Death? Then have no concern. I shall stride before you and your mouth will cry out, 'Forward, we fear nothing.' Then, should I fall, I will leave behind me a name that shall be forever remembered by men. They will say of me, 'It was Gilgamesh who has fallen in battle against Humbaba, the Fierce.' And, after my sons are born to my house and they climb upon your knee and say unto you, 'Tell to us all that you know of our father,' you may relate to them of my glorious exploits."

Enkidu opened his mouth and spoke these words unto Gilgamesh, "My friend, how can we venture into the Forest of Cedars? The Great God Enlil has empowered Humbaba to safeguard the Forest of Cedars and has made it his lot to terrify men. This is a journey which must not be undertaken. Humbaba is a creature which must not be beheld. His grasp is powerful. His roar is like unto the Great Deluge. From out of his mouth spew forth flames of fire and his breath is Death. He hears every rustle of grass in the Forest, though it be a thousand leagues distant. Who would dare venture into his Forest? Adad the Storm God is first and Humbaba is second. Who is there, even amongst the Gods, who would dare to assail Humbaba? To safeguard the Forest of Cedars, the Great God Enlil has appointed Humbaba to terrify men. Whosoever shall dare to enter into the Forest of Cedars is struck down with a fearful distemper."

Whereupon did Gilgamesh speak thus unto Enkidu, "Why, my friend, do you utter such tremulous words? Your speech does grieve me overmuch. It is not given to men to live forever. Numbered are their life-days, and all their exertions are but like the Wind. What has become of your strength and valor? You were born and reared in the wilderness. Even the lions feared you. All dangers have you encountered. Men fled before your presence. Undaunted was your courage. Why do you now falter? Come, let us journey together unto the Forest of Cedars. I will fell the Great Cedar Tree and gain Fame everlasting. Now must we hie to the forge. My charge to the armorers I fain would deliver, so they do cast our weapons in our presence."

And it came to pass that Gilgamesh did take Enkidu by the hand and carry him unto the place wherein the armorers abided. Then did Gilgamesh command the smiths to craft weapons for him. Whereupon, the smiths seated themselves to deliberate upon the matter. And then did the smiths craft mighty weapons, great axes weighing one hundred eighty pounds. Also great swords did they cast. Each blade had the weight of one hundred twenty pounds. The hilt thereof weighed thirty pounds and each sword was inlaid with thirty pounds of gold. With thirty score pounds of weapons was Gilgamesh laden. And with thirty score pounds of weapons was Enkidu laden.

And it befell that Gilgamesh did command his vassals to bolt shut the sevenfold gates of high-wall'd Uruk. The multitudes convened in the streets and in the market-place. The people assembled about Gilgamesh. Gilgamesh did seat himself upon his throne. The Elders of Uruk sat at the feet of Gilgamesh.

Whereupon did Gilgamesh address the Elders of Uruk thus, "Hear me, O Elders of high-ramparted Uruk. I go now unto the lair of Humbaba, the Fierce. I shall confront the monster of whom all men speak, the one whose renown is wide-spread in all the lands. I will overwhelm him in the Forest of Cedars and make manifest the might of the Son of Uruk. All the peoples of all the nations shall learn of my deeds of valor. I am determined to enter the Forest of Cedars and slay mighty Humbaba and fell the Great Cedar Tree, that I may attain Fame everlasting."

And then did Gilgamesh address the young men of Uruk thus, "Hear me, O young men of high-ramparted Uruk. You young men of Uruk know combat well, when, beside me, you did fight valiantly. Upon a distant road do I now travel to face Humbaba, the Fierce. I know not what Fate awaits me. Give me your blessing ere I embark on my journey, so I may once again behold your faces upon my joyous return unto the gate of high-wall'd Uruk. And then, upon my return, will I celebrate the Festival of the New Year with you. Indeed, I will celebrate the Festival of the New Year twice over. Then shall the merriment begin and the drums resound throughout all the city."

However, Enkidu did then utter these words unto the Elders of Uruk and the young men of Uruk who knew combat, "Tell Gilgamesh he must not go unto the Forest of Cedars. Tell him this is a journey which should not be undertaken. Humbaba, the Fierce is a monster who must not be beheld. To be feared is the Guardian of the Forest of Cedars. His roar is like unto the Great Deluge. From out of his mouth spew forth flames of fire and his breath is Death. He hears every rustle of grass in the Forest, though it be a thousand leagues distant. Who would dare venture into his Forest? Adad the Storm God is first and Humbaba is second. Who is there, even amongst the Gods, who would dare assail Humbaba? To safeguard the Forest of Cedars, the Great God Enlil has appointed Humbaba to terrify men. Whosoever shall dare to enter into the Forest of Cedars is struck down with a fearful distemper."

Then did the Elders of Uruk arise and speak unto Gilgamesh thus, "Gilgamesh, you are young. Your valor does overmuch mislead you. You know not what you seek to accomplish. It has come to our ears that Humbaba is not like mortals whose life-days are numbered. His weapons are such that none may withstand them. The length of the Forest of Cedars is ten thousand leagues and the breadth thereof is ten thousand leagues. Humbaba's roar is like unto the Great Deluge. From out of his mouth spew forth flames of fire and his breath is Death. He hears every rustle of grass in the Forest, though it be a thousand leagues distant. Who would dare venture into his Forest? Adad the Storm God is first and Humbaba is second. Who is there, even amongst the Gods, who would dare assail Humbaba? To safeguard the Forest of Cedars, the Great God Enlil has appointed Humbaba to terrify men."

Unto these words of the Elders of Uruk did Gilgamesh hearken. Whereupon did Gilgamesh turn his face toward Enkidu and laugh. Then Gilgamesh spoke these words unto Enkidu, "Shall I not fight Humbaba, the Fierce, because I am afraid of facing Death? Shall I be accounted a coward? I think not. It is only through deeds of glory that I will achieve eternal renown. To every warrior is Death preferable to Dishonor. Though I may dread Humbaba, yet shall I venture into the depths of the Forest of Cedars to confront him."

Tablet III

And then did the Elders of Uruk speak thus unto Gilgamesh, "May you return safely unto the sanctuary of high-wall'd Uruk. Trust not, O Gilgamesh, upon your strength alone. Be wary and watchful. Make your blow strike hard and true. The one who walks in front protects his comrade. The one who knows the way walks before the other and safeguards his friend. Let Enkidu go before you. The way unto the Forest of Cedars is known to Enkidu. He has seen battle and is practiced in the arts of combat. Enkidu will watch over his friend and safeguard his companion. Enkidu shall guide Gilgamesh safely home unto his beloved subjects. May the Gods protect you and lead you safely home unto high-wall'd Uruk."

Then the Elders of Uruk did address the following words unto Enkidu, "We, the Assembly of Elders of Uruk, do entrust our King Gilgamesh into your care. Upon your return, O Enkidu, you will once again restore him unto our care."

And it came to pass that Gilgamesh spoke thus unto Enkidu, "Come, my friend, let us betake ourselves to the Temple Sublime. Let us present ourselves before Ninsun, the Great Wild Cow Goddess. Ninsun is smart and all-knowing. Wise counsel will she render unto us for the road upon which we must travel."

Whereupon did Gilgamesh and Enkidu clasp their hands, each to the other, and go together unto the Temple Sublime to stand in the presence of Ninsun, the Great Wild Cow Goddess. Into the Temple Sublime did Gilgamesh enter first and stand before Ninsun, the Great Queen.

Gilgamesh spoke these words unto Ninsun, "I travel, O Ninsun, my mother, upon a distant road to the place wherein Humbaba abides. Unknown to me is the path I must take. Unknown to me is the outcome of the battle. Of you I beseech your blessing that I may behold your face once again upon my safe return. Pray for me that I may reach the Forest of Cedars and slay Humbaba the Fierce, and extirpate from the land the Evil that Shamash the Sun God hates. And pray for me that I may joyfully re-enter the gates of high-wall'd Uruk in triumph. Upon my return I shall celebrate the Festival of the New Year. Indeed, I will celebrate the Festival of the New Year twice over. Then shall the merriment begin and the drums resound throughout the city."

Ninsun, the Great Wild Cow Goddess, did attend carefully and with distress to the words of her son, Gilgamesh. Then she entered into her chamber and bathed herself with water of tamarisk and soapwort. Whereupon did she don a robe as befitted her body and jewels as befitted her breast. Upon her head did she then place a crown, and a sash about her waist.

Whereupon did Ninsun ascend the stairs unto the parapet upon the roof of the Temple Sublime, and there did she set an offering of incense upon the altar of Shamash, the Sun God. Then Ninsun raised her arms unto Shamash, and said, "O Shamash, wherefore have you afflicted my son, Gilgamesh, with so restless a heart? Now have you moved him to journey upon a distant road unto the place wherein Humbaba dwells. Gilgamesh must travel upon a path unknown and face a battle whose outcome is unknown. Therefore, O Shamash, I entreat you to watch over my son from the day he sets forth unto the Forest of Cedars and slays Humbaba the Fierce and extirpates from the land the Evil that you hate. Each day, as you traverse the arc of the sky, may Aya your Bride not fail to remind you, when day is done, to entrust my son's care unto the stars, those watchmen of the night. O Great Shamash, you awaken the herds to go forth, you illuminate the land with your radiant glow, the mountains shine with your brilliance, the Heavens grow bright, and the beasts of the wilderness behold your light.

"While Gilgamesh makes his perilous journey unto the Forest of Cedars, O Mighty Shamash, may the days be long and may the nights be short. May Gilgamesh gird his loins; may his stride be sure and his arms strong. At nightfall, let him pitch a safe camp for sleep. Let his slumber be untroubled. May Aya your Bride not fail to remind you. At the instant when Gilgamesh and Enkidu shall behold Humbaba, O Shamash, raise up mighty gale-winds against Humbaba. South Wind, North Wind, East Wind and West Wind. Raise up Torrential Wind, Cyclone Wind, Blasting Wind, Typhoon Wind, Tornado Wind, Tempest Wind, Dust-Storm Wind, Demon Wind and Whirlwind. Let rise thirteen winds, to blind Humbaba's vision. Then allow the weapons of Gilgamesh to strike Humbaba a fatal blow. Upon the death of Humbaba will your radiance shine bright and will Gilgamesh revere you once more. Your fleet-footed mules shall bear you onward to your tranquil throne. A comfortable bed for the night shall be laid out for you. The Gods, your brethren, will serve you tasty victuals to delight your senses. And Aya your Bride will wipe your visage with the fringe of her white garment."

And once again did Ninsun beseech Shamash with these words, "O Mighty Shamash, will not Gilgamesh be accepted by the Gods as one of them? Will he not share the Heavens with you? Will he not share a scepter and a crown with the Moon? Will he not be as wise as Ea, God of the Deep Waters? Will he not reign with Irnina over mankind? Will he not abide with Ningizzida, God of the Tree of Life, in the Land of No Return? I implore you, O Great Shamash, to succor my son and watch over him, that he may return safely from the Forest of Cedars."

Then did Ninsun, Wild Cow Goddess, who was smart and all-knowing, extinguish the burning incense. Ninsun, mother of Gilgamesh, descended from the roof of the Temple Sublime. Whereupon did Ninsun summon Enkidu to appear before her, and did utter these words unto him, "O mighty Enkidu, though you are not the issue of my womb, yet shall I proclaim that your offspring will belong to the sacred votaries of Gilgamesh, along with the Priestesses, the Temple harlots and the servants of the Temple."

And then did Ninsun place a bejeweled pendant about the neck of Enkidu and speak these words, "As the Priestesses take in a foundling and the Daughters of the Gods rear an orphan child, so do I herewith take Enkidu, whom I love, as mine own son. He shall be as a brother unto Gilgamesh. May Gilgamesh favor Enkidu with his brotherly love. As you both journey unto the Forest of Cedars, may the days be long and may the nights be short. May you gird your loins. May your stride be sure and your arm be strong. At nightfall, may you pitch a safe camp for sleep. May your slumber be untroubled. O Enkidu, I entreat you to watch over Gilgamesh, my son, and protect him and restore him safely unto me."

Whereupon did Enkidu utter these words, "I vow unto you that I shall watch over Gilgamesh, your son, and protect him and restore him safely unto you, or forfeit my life in doing so."

And it came to pass that Gilgamesh did then offer up a sacrifice unto Shamash the Sun God and was as a suppliant. Therefore Gilgamesh knelt before the altar of Shamash and uttered these words, "Here I present myself, O Great Shamash, and lift up my hands in entreaty unto you. I go to the Forest of Cedars to vanquish Humbaba the Fierce. I beseech you to spare my life, that I may safely return unto the ramparts of Uruk. Unfold your protection over me and let the omens be favorable."

Here it befell that tears streamed down the face of Gilgamesh. Whereupon did Gilgamesh speak these words, "I venture upon a road I have never traversed. I know not if I shall return but, if I am spared, I shall pay you due homage, and render magnificent offerings unto you, and praise, honor and extol your name. And I will build for you a great house of worship and a great throne for you to sit upon."

And then did the armorers deliver their weapons unto Gilgamesh and Enkidu. Monstrous were the axes the armorers brought and monstrous were the swords. A great bow and great fletched arrows in a quiver did they give unto the hand of Gilgamesh. Now were Gilgamesh and Enkidu armed with worthy weapons.

Whereupon did Gilgamesh instruct the Elders of Uruk concerning the affairs of the City, saying, "During the time of our journey unto the Forest of Cedars to slay Humbaba the Fierce, in order to extirpate from the land the Evil that Shamash hates, and until the time of our return unto high-wall'd Uruk, let not the youths gather in the street to form an assemblage, for much discord and unrest will they cause. Judge fairly the grievances and petitions of the weak and poor, and let not the strong and wealthy gain unjust advantage. Meanwhile we shall undertake to fulfill our Destiny and in Humbaba's breast impale our weapons."

Now the Elders of Uruk did arise and wish them well. The young men of Uruk paid them tribute. The people of Uruk did offer obeisance unto the two heroes. And then the Elders of Uruk blessed them and spoke thus, "Unto the sanctuary of high-wall'd Uruk we pray you return safely. Trust not, O Gilgamesh, upon your strength alone. Be wary and watchful. Make your blow strike hard and true. The one who walks in front protects his comrade. The one who knows the way walks before the other and safeguards his friend. Let Enkidu go before you. The way unto the Forest of Cedars is known to Enkidu. He has seen battle and is practiced in the arts of combat. Enkidu will watch over his friend and safeguard his companion. Enkidu shall guide Gilgamesh safely home unto his beloved subjects. May the Gods protect you and lead you safely home unto high-wall'd Uruk."

Then the Elders of Uruk did address the following words unto Enkidu, "We, the Assembly of Elders of Uruk, do entrust our King Gilgamesh into your care. Upon your return, O Enkidu, you will once again restore him unto our care."

But now did the eyes of Enkidu fill with tears and now was Enkidu's heart heavy as he uttered these words unto Gilgamesh, "Turn back, my friend. Pursue not this perilous journey whose outcome is uncertain. I am afeared for your safety."

But Gilgamesh heeded not this counsel of Enkidu. He took up the mighty weapons which had been fashioned for him. Gilgamesh set his hand upon the great sword and the great bow and the fletched arrows in their quiver. Over his shoulder did he sling the great bow and the fletched arrows in their quiver. Upon his belt did he hang the great sword and in his hand did he carry the great axe.

And now did the Elders of Uruk offer this supplication in aid of Gilgamesh, "May Shamash the Sun God grant you success in your endeavor. May He grant that your eyes witness the consummation of the words of your utterance. May He open for you the path that is blocked. May He cleave a road that you may tread upon it. May He level the uplands for your feet. May nightfall gladden you and may King Lugalbanda, your father, stand beside you and shelter you in your quest. May your triumph be swift. And, after you have overthrown Humbaba the Fierce, wash then your feet in his river as you exult in your victory. That night, as you repose, dig a well, that you might always have pure water in your water-skin. Then offer up a libation unto Shamash and forget not King Lugalbanda, your father."

Then did Enkidu speak these words unto Gilgamesh, "Since you have set your mind to make this foray, let not your heart be fearful. Let your footfalls follow mine. I know of the place wherein Humbaba abides and I know of the paths upon which he walks. Follow me that we may fulfill our Destiny."

When the Elders of Uruk heard this utterance, a great cry of acclaim arose. Whereupon did the people bid the heroes a safe journey with these words, "Go, Gilgamesh, and may the Gods accompany you. May Shamash watch over you and help you attain your heart's desire. May Shamash carry you safely home unto high-wall'd Uruk."

And then did Gilgamesh and Enkidu go forth.

Tablet IV

At twenty leagues did Gilgamesh and Enkidu break bread. At thirty leagues did they repose for the night. Fifty leagues did they traverse in a day. In the space of three days did Gilgamesh and Enkidu traverse a journey of seven weeks. Whereupon did they draw yet nearer unto Mount Lebanon. Facing Shamash the Sun God as He set, they dug a well, from which they filled their water-skins with fresh water. And then did Gilgamesh ascend to the mountain peak, where he poured out upon the ground an enchanted circle of milled flour as an offering, and uttered these words in supplication, "O Mountain, bring unto me a dream, that I may receive a favorable sign from Shamash."

And it befell that Enkidu built for Gilgamesh a dwelling for the God of Dreams. Unto this dwelling did Enkidu affix a door, that the wind might not enter therein. Then did Enkidu bid Gilgamesh to lie upon the ground, so he could pour about him an enchanted circle of milled flour to cause Gilgamesh to dream. And then did Enkidu betake himself to lie upon the threshold of the dwelling.

In the night, Gilgamesh sat with his chin upon his knee. And, then, sleep came to him, as it does to all men. In the middle of the night, he ended his slumber. Gilgamesh arose and spoke unto his friend. These words did he speak unto Enkidu, "My friend, did you not call out to me? Why have I awakened? Did you not touch me? Why am I uneasy? Did a God not pass by? Why does my flesh tremble? Enkidu, my friend, I had a dream. The dream I had filled me with terror. I walked through a valley beneath a great mountain. The mountain fell down upon me. Under the mountain was I helpless and bereft of hope. And then did the Sun rise and cast its light over the mountain. O Enkidu, you who were begotten in the wilderness, relate unto me the import of this dream."

Enkidu, who was begotten in the wilderness, knew how to interpret dreams. He spoke unto Gilgamesh, his friend, and explained the meaning of the dream. Enkidu uttered these words, "My friend, your dream is auspicious. Your dream is meaningful to us and bodes well. The mountain you espied was Humbaba. Your dream signifies that we shall capture Humbaba and slay him. We shall hurl down his corpse upon the field of combat. And then, at the dawning, will we view a favorable sign from Shamash the Sun God."

And it came to pass that they journeyed onward. At twenty leagues did Gilgamesh and Enkidu break bread. At thirty leagues did they repose for the night. Fifty leagues did they traverse in a day. In the space of three days did Gilgamesh and Enkidu traverse a journey of seven weeks. Whereupon did they draw yet nearer unto Mount Lebanon. Facing Shamash the Sun God as he set, they dug a well, from which they filled their water-skins with fresh water. And then did Gilgamesh ascend to the mountain peak, where he poured out upon the ground an enchanted circle of milled flour as an offering, and uttered these words in supplication, "O Mountain, bring unto me a dream, that I may receive a favorable sign from Shamash."

And it befell that Enkidu built for Gilgamesh a dwelling for the God of Dreams. Unto this dwelling did Enkidu affix a door, that the wind might not enter therein. Then did Enkidu bid Gilgamesh to lie upon the ground, so he could pour about him an enchanted circle of milled flour to cause Gilgamesh to dream. And then did Enkidu betake himself to lie upon the threshold of the dwelling.

In the night, Gilgamesh sat with his chin upon his knee. And, then, sleep came to him, as it does to all men. In the middle of the night, he ended his slumber. Gilgamesh arose and spoke unto his friend. These words did he speak unto Enkidu, "My friend, did you not call out to me? Why have I awakened? Did you not touch me? Why am I uneasy? Did a God not pass by? Why does my flesh tremble? Enkidu, my friend, I had a second dream. This dream surpasses the first in terror. In my dream, the mountain appeared before me. Then the mountain threw me down. By my feet did the mountain grasp me and hold me fast. Whereupon, a fearsome brilliance did appear over the land and did grow ever brighter. And then a man appeared with the most comely features in all the land, his beauty unsurpassed. From the grip of the mountain did this man free me. He gave me water to drink. My heart grew placid. Upon the ground did he place my feet once again. O Enkidu, you who were begotten in the wilderness, relate unto me the import of this dream."

Enkidu, who was begotten in the wilderness, knew how to interpret dreams. He spoke unto Gilgamesh, his friend, and explained the meaning of the dream. Enkidu uttered these words, "My friend, your dream is favorable to us. The mountain you espied is Humbaba. He did throw you down and grasp you by the feet. But the comely man who succored you was Shamash the Sun God, who will assist us in our quest. Therefore, banish your fear and let us resume our journey."

And it came to pass that they journeyed onward. At twenty leagues did Gilgamesh and Enkidu break bread. At thirty leagues did they repose for the night. Fifty leagues did they traverse in a day. In the space of three days did Gilgamesh and Enkidu traverse a journey of seven weeks. Whereupon did they draw yet nearer unto Mount Lebanon. Facing Shamash the Sun God as he set, they dug a well, from which they filled their water-skins with fresh water. And then did Gilgamesh ascend to the mountain peak, where he poured out upon the ground an enchanted circle of milled flour as an offering, and uttered these words in supplication, "O Mountain, bring unto me a dream, that I may receive a favorable sign from Shamash."

And it befell that Enkidu built for Gilgamesh a dwelling for the God of Dreams. Unto this dwelling did Enkidu affix a door, that the wind might not enter therein. Then did Enkidu bid Gilgamesh to lie upon the ground, so he could pour about him an enchanted circle of milled flour to cause Gilgamesh to dream. And then did Enkidu betake himself to lie upon the threshold of the dwelling.

In the night, Gilgamesh sat with his chin upon his knee. And, then, sleep came to him, as it does to all men. In the middle of the night, he ended his slumber. Gilgamesh arose and spoke unto his friend. These words did he speak unto Enkidu, "My friend, did you not call out to me? Why have I awakened? Did you not touch me? Why am I uneasy? Did a God not pass by? Why does my flesh tremble? Enkidu, my friend, I had a third dream. This dream surpasses the first two in terror. In my dream the Heavens roared aloud and the Earth rumbled. Daylight failed and the darkness fell over all. Then lightning flashed and fire blazed forth. And then the flames did burgeon and flare up, and Death did then rain down. Whereupon, the brightness was dimmed and the flames were extinguished. And all was covered by cinders and ashes. O Enkidu, you who were begotten in the wilderness, relate unto me the import of this dream."

Enkidu, who was begotten in the wilderness, knew how to interpret dreams. He spoke unto Gilgamesh, his friend, and explained the meaning of the dream. Enkidu uttered these words, "My friend, your dream is favorable to us. The lightning and flames of which you speak is Humbaba the Fierce. Humbaba tried, but was unable, to vanquish you, whereupon his brightness was dimmed, and he was covered by cinders and ashes. This means we shall prevail over him and slay him. We approach ever closer unto the Forest of Cedars. The hour of battle draws near."

And it came to pass that they journeyed onward. At twenty leagues did Gilgamesh and Enkidu break bread. At thirty leagues did they repose for the night. Fifty leagues did they traverse in a day. In the space of three days did Gilgamesh and Enkidu traverse a journey of seven weeks. Whereupon did they draw yet nearer unto Mount Lebanon. Facing Shamash the Sun God as he set, they dug a well, from which they filled their water-skins with fresh water. And then did Gilgamesh ascend to the mountain peak, where he poured out upon the ground an enchanted circle of milled flour as an offering, and uttered these words in supplication, "O Mountain, bring unto me a dream, that I may receive a favorable sign from Shamash."

And it befell that Enkidu built for Gilgamesh a dwelling for the God of Dreams. Unto this dwelling did Enkidu affix a door, that the wind might not enter therein. Then did Enkidu bid Gilgamesh to lie upon the ground, so he could pour about him an enchanted circle of milled flour to cause Gilgamesh to dream. And then did Enkidu betake himself to lie upon the threshold of the dwelling.

In the night, Gilgamesh sat with his chin upon his knee. And, then, sleep came to him, as it does to all men. In the middle of the night, he ended his slumber. Gilgamesh arose and spoke unto his friend. These words did he speak unto Enkidu, "My friend, did you not call out to me? Why have I awakened? Did you not touch me? Why am I uneasy? Did a God not pass by? Why does my flesh tremble? Enkidu, my friend, I had a fourth dream. This dream surpasses the first three in terror. In my dream I beheld the great lion-headed eagle God Anzu in the sky. It soared above me like a cloud. Toward me it began to descend. Its appearance was dreadful. Its visage evoked horror. Huge flames shot forth from out of its mouth. Its breath was Death. Then I beheld a man standing by my side in my dream. He seized the great lion-headed eagle God Anzu by the wings and did cast it down upon the ground before me. O Enkidu, you who were begotten in the wilderness, relate unto me the import of this dream."

Enkidu, who was begotten in the wilderness, knew how to interpret dreams. He spoke unto Gilgamesh, his friend, and explained the meaning of the dream. Enkidu uttered these words, "My friend, your dream is favorable to us. In your dream you beheld the great lion-headed eagle God Anzu in the sky. It soared above you like a cloud. Toward you it began to descend. Its appearance was dreadful. Its visage evoked horror. Huge flames shot forth from out of its mouth. Its breath was Death. Then you beheld a man standing by your side in your dream. He seized the great lion-headed eagle God Anzu by the wings and did cast it down upon the ground before you. My friend, the man you perceived was mighty Shamash the Sun God. As He subdued the great lion-headed eagle God Anzu, will He subdue Humbaba the Fierce. As He seized the wings of the great lion-headed eagle God Anzu will He seize the arms of Humbaba the Fierce that we may slay him. And, the morning following, we shall observe a good sign from Shamash the Sun God."

And it came to pass that they journeyed onward. At twenty leagues did Gilgamesh and Enkidu break bread. At thirty leagues did they repose for the night. Fifty leagues did they traverse in a day. In the space of three days did Gilgamesh and Enkidu traverse a journey of seven weeks. Whereupon did they draw yet nearer unto Mount Lebanon. Facing Shamash the Sun God as he set, they dug a well, from which they filled their water-skins with fresh water. And then did Gilgamesh ascend to the mountain peak, where he poured out upon the ground an enchanted circle of milled flour as an offering, and uttered these words in supplication, "O Mountain, bring unto me a dream, that I may receive a favorable sign from Shamash."

And it befell that Enkidu built for Gilgamesh a dwelling for the God of Dreams. Unto this dwelling did Enkidu affix a door, that the wind might not enter therein. Then did Enkidu bid Gilgamesh to lie upon the ground, so he could pour about him an enchanted circle of milled flour to cause Gilgamesh to dream. And then did Enkidu betake himself to lie upon the threshold of the dwelling.

In the night, Gilgamesh sat with his chin upon his knee. And, then, sleep came to him, as it does to all men. In the middle of the night, he ended his slumber. Gilgamesh arose and spoke unto his friend. These words did he speak unto Enkidu, "My friend, did you not call out to me? Why have I awakened? Did you not touch me? Why am I uneasy? Did a God not pass by? Why does my flesh tremble? Enkidu, my friend, I had a fifth dream. This dream surpasses the first four in terror. This dream filled me with bewilderment and dread. In my dream, I grappled with a huge wild bull. As it bellowed, its hooves pounded the Earth and raised great clouds of dust that darkened the Firmament. I fell before this huge wild bull. My strength was unequal to the task and I was unable to move. Then a man raised me up by mine arms and touched my cheek. This man gave me water to drink from his water-skin. O Enkidu, you who were begotten in the wilderness, relate unto me the import of this dream."

Enkidu, who was begotten in the wilderness, knew how to interpret dreams. He spoke unto Gilgamesh, his friend, and explained the meaning of the dream. Enkidu uttered these words, "My friend, your dream is favorable to us. The huge wild bull with whom you grappled is not our adversary. The huge wild bull with whom you grappled is Shamash, our Protector. In time of peril, He will take our hand. And the one who gave you water to drink from his water-skin is your own God, your father, Lugalbanda. He will join with us to accomplish a feat greater than any which has ever been heard of in all the land."

And it came to pass that Gilgamesh and Enkidu journeyed onward until, at last, they reached the Forest of Cedars. Whereupon did Gilgamesh desist and hesitate before entering into the Forest of Cedars. And then did Gilgamesh weep, and his tears did flow copiously down his face.

At this, Enkidu spoke to Gilgamesh in this manner, "Wherefore, my friend, do you weep and do your tears flow? O worthy scion, sprung from the womb of high-wall'd Uruk, do now stand resolute in the face of your foe, Humbaba the Fierce. Stand tall and unyielding, O Gilgamesh, my King, sprung from the womb of Uruk of the mighty ramparts."

Shamash the Sun God gave ear to these words. Then, from the Heavens, issued forth this pronouncement in a thunderous voice from the mouth of Shamash, "Hasten at once. Go forward and assail Humbaba. Let him not enter into the depths of the Forest of Cedars. Let him not wrap himself in the seven enchanted cloaks which afford him protection. He has donned one, but he has shed the other six. Now is he vulnerable. Propitious now is the moment to assault him."

Gilgamesh heard these words of Shamash and his heart was emboldened. Gilgamesh charged forward like unto a raging wild bull. He roared out the bellow of a raging wild bull. Onward did Gilgamesh and Enkidu venture unto the Forest of Cedars.

Tablet V

And Gilgamesh and Enkidu stood unmoving before the Forest of Cedars. They spoke not. At the height of the Cedar Tree did they marvel. They espied the way into the Forest of Cedars and the path upon which Humbaba the Fierce was wont to tread. The road was straight and well-trodden. They perceived the Mountain of Cedar, the Dwelling Place of the Gods and the Throne of Ishtar. Upon the face of the Mountain of Cedar the trees grew in abundance. The shade of the trees was good and agreeable withal. Beneath the trees the undergrowth was entangled with thorn-bushes, with thickets interwoven.

And it came to pass that Enkidu's heart did tremble and his spirit did falter, and he spoke these words unto Gilgamesh, "My friend, I am afeared. Let us go not into the depths of the Forest of Cedars. When I drew near the path into the Forest of Cedars, forsooth, the strength did depart from mine arms and my hands did grow weak. Let us venture no further onward. You know not this monster and thus you fear him not. I know him and I fear him. Like a dragon's fangs are his teeth. His countenance is like unto that of a lion. His assault is like the onslaught of a mighty flood, which overwhelms the trees of the forest and the undergrowth of the wilderness in its path."

Then did Gilgamesh answer Enkidu thus, "My friend, why speak you like a coward? Have we not traversed many mountains together? The end of our quest is near unto us. My friend, you who have seen battle, you who are practiced in the arts of warfare, stand by my side and you shall not fear Death. Let your cry resound like the bellow of a wild bull. And then will the strength return unto your arms and the weakness will leave your hands. Take my hand, my friend, and let us journey onward to fulfill our Destiny. One of us alone cannot slay Humbaba. Together, our might cannot be matched, just as the rope with three strands cannot be broken. Allow your heart to grow eager for combat. The one who walks in front protects himself and defends his comrade. Forever will our valor be spoken of in the encampments of brave-hearted men."

And then did they continue on and arrive at their journey's end. Whereupon did they cease their discourse and halt at that place. Then did Gilgamesh and Enkidu draw forth their weapons. They unsheathed their mighty swords from the scabbards and whet their great axes upon the whetstones. And then did they stride forward to confront Humbaba the Fierce.

Whereupon did Humbaba the Fierce emerge from his stronghold of Cedar. And Gilgamesh and Enkidu lifted up their eyes and beheld Humbaba the Fierce.

His countenance was fearsome and terrible to behold. Humbaba made ready to speak unto Gilgamesh, and uttered these words, "You are a fool, Gilgamesh, to take counsel from this rude and brutish creature who accompanies you. Why do you venture hither unto my presence? Come, Enkidu, you spawn of a fish, who knows of no father. Come, Enkidu, you brood of a tortoise, who suckled of no mother's milk. When you were but a youngling, I did observe you, and went near you not. Had I killed you then and eaten you, would you have filled my belly? Now, in perfidy, do you bring Gilgamesh to stand before me. Now, Enkidu, do you stand before me in warlike aspect. I shall rip asunder the throat of Gilgamesh and sever his head from his neck. Unto the ravenous raven, the screeching eagle and the cawing vulture shall I feed his flesh."

At these words of Humbaba did Gilgamesh speak thus unto Enkidu, "My friend, Humbaba's countenance does grow ever more monstrous. Although we did stride like heroes into the Forest of Cedars to vanquish Humbaba, now does my heart beat faster and my courage slacken."

Whereupon did Enkidu utter these words unto Gilgamesh, "Why, my friend, speak you like one who is afeared? Unworthy of a great King is your speech. Your words do grieve me. The time to strike is now. The copper has already been poured into the mold to fashion our weapons. Will you take an hour to blow the bellows for the furnace? Will you take another hour for the metal to cool? Now is the moment to unleash the Flood. Now is the moment to crack the Whip. Retreat not a step. Do not turn back. Now is the time to strike a mighty blow."

Gilgamesh heeded the words of Enkidu and his courage returned unto him. Whereupon did Gilgamesh cry out to Shamash the Sun God, "O Great Shamash, I offer my prayers in entreaty unto you. I did set out upon the road as you ordained in order to do your bidding. Now do I beseech you to succor me in this, my battle against Humbaba the Fierce."

And it came to pass that Gilgamesh and Enkidu did then assail Humbaba. As they joined battle, the three warriors smote the ground with their feet and the Earth did burst asunder. Mount Hermon split apart from Mount Lebanon. White clouds did turn black. Death rained down upon them like unto a fog. Whereupon did Shamash the Sun God hearken unto the entreaty of Gilgamesh. Against Humbaba did Shamash the Sun God raise up mighty-gale winds. Yea, a great wind from the North did Shamash raise. Likewise did He raise up South Wind, East Wind and West Wind. Likewise did Shamash raise up Torrential Wind, Cyclone Wind, Blasting Wind, Typhoon Wind, Tornado Wind, Tempest Wind, Dust-Storm Wind, Demon Wind and Whirlwind. Shamash let rise thirteen winds to blind Humbaba's vision. And it befell that Humbaba was not able to charge forward. Neither was Humbaba able to retreat. And now did Gilgamesh's weapons defeat and overthrow Humbaba.

Humbaba was vanquished. Wherefore, to Gilgamesh did Humbaba offer this plea to spare his life, "You are yet young, Gilgamesh. Your mother not so long ago gave birth to you. The true offspring of Ninsun the Wild Cow Goddess are you. It is hereby manifest that you have fulfilled the prophesy of Shamash, Lord of the Mountain, to triumph over me. O Gilgamesh, scion of high-wall'd Uruk, you are verily a great and mighty King. I beg you to stay your hand. A dead creature cannot serve his master. You shall be my master and I shall be your servant. Let me continue to dwell here in the Forest of Cedars, and I will fell for you as many trees as you desire. For you will I construct the most proud Palace of Cedar, one that will be spoken of by men for ages to come."

At this, Enkidu made reply unto Gilgamesh in this manner, "My friend, heed not this entreaty of Humbaba. Listen in nowise to his supplications."

But then Humbaba spoke thus unto Enkidu, "You, Enkidu, have knowledge of the lore of my Forest and you understand all that I affirm. You should know that Enlil, God of Earth, Wind and Air, made me Guardian of the Forest of Cedars, and bestowed upon me this horrible aspect in order to terrify men. Harken unto my words. I might have seized you and hanged you from a tree at the entrance to the Forest of Cedars. I might have fed your flesh to the ravenous raven, the screeching eagle and the cawing vulture, but I did not. So now, Enkidu, my deliverance depends upon your goodwill. I beseech you to tell Gilgamesh to spare my life."

Whereupon did Enkidu speak these words unto Gilgamesh, "My friend, delay not, but hasten to slay Humbaba, Guardian of the Forest of Cedars. Swiftly kill him, destroy him, vanquish his power. Delay not, but hasten to slay Humbaba, Guardian of the Forest of Cedars. Swiftly kill him, destroy him, vanquish his power, before Enlil, God of Earth, Wind and Air, hears of what we do, and the Great Gods become enraged against us, Enlil in Nippur, Shamash in Larsa. Establish for all time your renown among men, of how Gilgamesh slew Humbaba the Fierce in the Forest of Cedars."

Humbaba gave ear to the words of Enkidu and raised his head to speak thus, "Enkidu, you sit like a shepherd at the feet of Gilgamesh. Before Gilgamesh do you sit, like a hireling doing his bidding. Now, Enkidu, I do beg for clemency. Bid Gilgamesh spare my life."

And these words did Enkidu say unto Gilgamesh, "My friend, delay not, but hasten to slay Humbaba, Guardian of the Forest of Cedars. Swiftly kill him, destroy him, vanquish his power. Delay not, but hasten to slay Humbaba, Guardian of the Forest of Cedars. Swiftly kill him, destroy him, vanquish his power, before Enlil, God of Earth, Wind and Air, hears of what we do, and the Great Gods become enraged against us, Enlil in Nippur, Shamash in Larsa. Establish for all time your renown among men, of how Gilgamesh slew Humbaba the Fierce in the Forest of Cedars."

Now did Humbaba hear these words and understand that the end of his life-days was at hand. Whereupon Humbaba did impart his curse unto Gilgamesh and Enkidu, saying, "May the two of you never enjoy a good old age. May Enkidu die before Gilgamesh, who, stricken with grief, shall bury his friend. I lay this, my curse, upon you."

Gilgamesh lowered his sword, dismayed by the curse of Humbaba, but Enkidu now uttered these words, "My friend, I speak to you but you hear me not. You hear only the curse of Humbaba. Give no credence to his curse. Let his curse return unto his mouth, from whence it came. Strike now, and smite Humbaba."

Gilgamesh gave heed to these words of his friend. He raised his sword and smote Humbaba with a mighty blow to the neck. And then did Enkidu strike a second mighty blow against Humbaba. At the third blow did Humbaba fall.

Now was Humbaba slain, the Guardian of the Forest of Cedars. And now did the ravines run red with the life-blood of Humbaba, and for the space of two leagues around did the Cedars resound. Humbaba was slain, he whose roar made Mount Hermon and Mount Lebanon tremble. And now did all the mountains quake and all the hillsides shake. Now did rain fall in abundance onto the mountains. Whereupon did Gilgamesh and Enkidu slice open Humbaba and remove his entrails. And now did Gilgamesh and Enkidu sever the head of Humbaba from his body.

And it came to pass that Gilgamesh took up his mighty axe and entered into the Sacred Dwelling of the Gods. Therein did Gilgamesh fell the tall Trees of Cedar whilst Enkidu did hew the Trees into lumber. Then did Enkidu speak thus unto Gilgamesh, "My friend, you have slain Humbaba by means of your great strength and valor. By your might did you fell the tall Trees of Cedar. Who could doubt your glory now? You have cut down the lofty Cedar whose crown once pierced the Heavens. I shall craft from it a door seventy-two cubits in height and twenty-four cubits in width and one cubit in thickness. No mortal may pass through this door. Only a God shall be able to enter through it. Along the river Euphrates will we sail this Sacred Door unto the sanctuary of the Great God Enlil in Nippur. There will the men of Nippur rejoice in it. And there will the Great God Enlil delight in it."

When Gilgamesh and Enkidu had accomplished this, they lashed together a great raft of Cedar and laid the Sacred Door upon it. Whereupon did they sail down the river Euphrates toward Nippur. Enkidu was the helmsman and Gilgamesh bore, in his arms, the head of Humbaba.

Tablet VI

In high-wall'd Uruk did Gilgamesh wash his matted hair and shake his locks loose over his shoulders. He bathed and cast aside his besmirched garments and donned clean apparel. In regal attire did he clothe himself, and gird himself about the waist with a sash. And then did Gilgamesh place his crown upon his head.

When Ishtar, Goddess of Love and Fertility, espied the comeliness of Gilgamesh, she was overcome with longing, and did say, "Come unto me, Gilgamesh, and be my bridegroom. Fill my womb with your seed. Be my husband and I shall be your wife. For you will I harness a chariot of lapis lazuli and gold, with wheels of gold and yoke of amber. This chariot shall be drawn by a team of storm-demons, in the stead of draft mules. When you enter into our Temple with the sweet fragrance of Cedarwood, the most excellent Purification Priests will kiss your feet. Kings, nobles and sovereigns will bend the knee before you. Unto you shall they render tribute from mountain and lowland. Your she-goats shall bear triplets and your ewes shall bear twins. Your burden-laden donkey will outrace the unencumbered mule. Your oxen under the yoke shall have no match. And your chariot steeds will garner renown for their swiftness."

Gilgamesh made reply unto the Goddess Ishtar in this manner, "Aye, but what shall I grant you if I take you to wife? Must I provide you with perfumed unguents for your body and fine raiment with which to clothe yourself? Would I offer you bread and victual, you who eat the food of the Gods? You who drink wine meet for a King? What would be my advantage if I should take you in marriage? You are like unto a fire that goes out in the cold, a door that keeps out neither windstorm nor tempest, a palace that collapses upon those within, pitch that blackens the hand of the workman, a water-skin that holds not water, a weak limestone foundation that undermines the rampart, a battering ram that fails against a foe, and a sandal that causes the wearer to trip and fall. Who of your husbands did you faithfully love for all time? Who of your little shepherds held your affection for many seasons?

"Forsooth, I shall now recount unto you the litany of your lovers. First was Tammuz, the consort of your maidenhead. You raised him from mere mortal to a Divine. But you sent him to his doom in the Netherworld and, for year after year, have you decreed wailing in lamentation for him. Then comes next the gay-feathered Roller bird. You loved him, but struck him and broke his wing. Now, upon a branch in his grove of trees, does he sit and cry, 'My wing, my wing.' Loved you also the lion, unsurpassed in strength. Yet you did dig for him seven pits and again seven pits to entrap him. Loved you also the stallion, splendid War Horse. But you commanded for him the lash, the bridle and the spur. You ordained that he should gallop without pause for seven leagues and slake his thirst from muddied waters. And to his mother Silili, the Divine Mare, did you give cause for eternal weeping. The Shepherd of the Flock did you love. He baked for you bread each day. And each day would he slaughter a kid for you. But you smote him and transformed him into a wolf. And now his own herd boys harry him away from the flock, and his own dogs snap at his flanks. Loved you also Ishullanu, the gardener who tended your father's date-groves. He would bring you endless baskets of dates. Every day would he garnish your table with delectable viands. When you cast your eyes upon him, you were smitten with lust. You went unto him and said, 'O my Ishullanu, let me taste of your member. Put forth your hand and caress my loins.' But Ishullanu replied unto you, 'Me? What is it you want of me? Has my mother not baked and have I not eaten? Why should I now eat of the bread of transgression? Why should I now eat of the bread of iniquity? And should a blanket of reeds be my only protection against the winter's cold?' When you gave ear to his words, you struck him and transformed him into a frog and made him dwell in his own date-grove, from which he cannot move nor depart. And now, since you love me, am I doomed to suffer the same Fate as the others?"

When these words the Goddess Ishtar heard, her choler was inflamed and she grew exceeding wrathful. In a fury did she fly upward unto Heaven. She hied herself before her father Anu, Lord of the Gods, and her mother, Antu, where she wept bitter tears. And Ishtar did then speak these words, "O Father, again and again does Gilgamesh disdain me. Slanderous words has he uttered about me. He does insult me with despicable imprecations."

Whereupon did Anu make reply unto Ishtar in this manner, "Daughter, did you not provoke King Gilgamesh? Hence has he disdained you and uttered slanderous words about you and insulted you with despicable imprecations."

And Ishtar spoke unto Anu thus, "Father, I beseech you, grant me the Bull of Heaven, that I may vanquish Gilgamesh where he abides. Let the Bull of Heaven gorge himself upon Gilgamesh where he abides. If you give me not the Bull of Heaven, I shall tear down the Gates of the Netherworld and raise up the Dead to devour the Living. And the Dead shall outnumber the Living, and they shall consume the flesh of the Living."

Anu, Lord of the Gods, made answer unto Ishtar thus, "If you ask of me the Bull of Heaven, and I unleash it, then will there be seven years of drought in the land of Uruk. For seven lean years will the farmer harvest only chaff and empty husks. Have you gathered sufficient grain for the populace? And have you gathered sufficient provender for the cattle?"

Ishtar spoke these words unto Anu, her father, "I have already stored up sufficient grain for the populace. I have already stored up sufficient provender for the cattle. Against seven lean years have I husbanded sufficient foodstuffs for the populace and sufficient fodder for the cattle. Now render unto me the Bull of Heaven. With the wrath of the Bull of Heaven shall I slay Gilgamesh."

When Anu heard these words of Ishtar, he did place in her hand the nose rope of the Bull of Heaven. Whereupon did Ishtar descend with the Bull of Heaven unto the gates of high-wall'd Uruk. And then did the Bull of Heaven drink up the waters upon the face of the Earth, and then did the groves and the reed-beds and the marshlands dry up. Then did the Bull of Heaven drink from the river Euphrates and cause the level of the water to fall by the height of seven cubits. When the Bull of Heaven snorted, the ground cracked open and a hundred men of Uruk fell to their death therein. The Bull of Heaven snorted a second time, and the ground cracked open and two hundred men of Uruk fell to their death therein. And then did the Bull of Heaven snort a third time, whereupon the ground cracked open and Enkidu did fall therein up to his middle. But Enkidu did swiftly leap out and seize the Bull of Heaven by its horns. Whereupon did the Bull of Heaven spit its saliva upon Enkidu and splay its dung upon Enkidu with the swish of its tail.

And Enkidu did say unto Gilgamesh, "My friend, we avowed that we would gain renown and glory everlasting. Now must we show the people that we are capable of great and valorous accomplishments by vanquishing the mighty Bull of Heaven. I have witnessed the strength of the Bull of Heaven. I know its strength and I know its weakness. The Bull of Heaven I know how to destroy. I shall go behind the Bull of Heaven and seize it by the thick of its tail. Then shall I place my foot upon the back of its haunch. And then must you, like a valiant and skilled slaughterer, thrust your sword between the nape of the neck and the horns."

And it befell that Enkidu did then go behind the Bull of Heaven and did seize it by the thick of its tail. Then Enkidu placed his foot upon the back of the haunch of the Bull of Heaven. And then did Gilgamesh, like a valiant and skilled slaughterer, thrust his sword between the nape of the neck and the horns of the Bull of Heaven. Whereupon did the Bull of Heaven fall dead.

And, after Gilgamesh and Enkidu had slain the Bull of Heaven, they did tear out its heart and bear it up unto Shamash, the Sun God. They did bear up the heart of the Bull of Heaven and set it before Shamash in an offering of sacrifice. Then did Gilgamesh and Enkidu step back and prostrate themselves before Shamash. Whereupon, they did then take their repose and sit themselves, side by side, like unto brethren.

But then Goddess Ishtar mounted the crest of the ramparts of high-wall'd Uruk. Unto the roof-top did Ishtar ascend and there did give voice to her wailing. Ishtar bemoaned and bewailed and lamented aloud her grief. And then did she hurl a curse thus, "Woe be unto Gilgamesh, who scorned me and slew the Bull of Heaven."

Upon hearing her words, Enkidu did rip off the hindquarter of the Bull of Heaven and did hurl it into the face of Ishtar and said, "If I could but lay mine hand upon you, this is how I would treat you. And, over your arm, would I hang the entrails of the Bull of Heaven."

At this, Ishtar, Goddess of Love and Fertility, assembled her minions, the Cult Priestesses, the Temple Harlots, the Shrine Courtesans. Over the hindquarter of the Bull of Heaven did they begin to chant the Rites of Lamentation.

And it came to pass that Gilgamesh commanded to appear before him the masters of craft and artisans of Uruk, all of them together. And they all marveled at the size of the horns of the Bull of Heaven. Each horn was fashioned from thirty pounds of lapis lazuli and the wall of each horn was the width of two thumbs in thickness. Six measures of oil was the capacity of both horns. Unto his Guardian God and father Lugalbanda did Gilgamesh offer the horns of the Bull of Heaven, to hold holy ointments for his devotional anointment. And Gilgamesh placed the horns of the Bull of Heaven upon the shrine of his forbears.

And now did Gilgamesh and Enkidu lave their hands in the river Euphrates. Then, arm in arm, they strode through the streets of Uruk. The multitudes gathered in the public places to gaze upon the heroes. Whereupon did Gilgamesh call out to the serving girls of his palace, "Who is the most winsome of men? Who is the most glorious of warriors?"

The serving girls of his palace did make reply thus, "Gilgamesh is the most winsome of men. Gilgamesh is the most glorious of warriors. And Enkidu, in his wrath, did rip off the hindquarter of the Bull of Heaven and did hurl it into the face of Ishtar, and now does Ishtar have no champion in the street to avenge her."

Whereupon was there feasting and mirth-making and the joy of revelry in the palace. And then did they retire unto their chambers to slumber for the night. Enkidu, while he slept, had a dream. Enkidu awoke and went unto his friend, Gilgamesh, to relate his dream.

Tablet VII

Enkidu spoke unto Gilgamesh thus, "My friend, I have had a dream. In my dream, the Great Gods met in council together. The Gods Anu, Enlil, Ea and Shamash were assembled. Whereupon did Anu, Lord of the Gods, say unto Enlil, God of Earth, Wind and Air, 'By reason that Gilgamesh and Enkidu have killed the Bull of Heaven and because they have slain Humbaba, Guardian of the Forest of Cedars, one of the twain must die.'

"Whereupon did Enlil make reply unto Anu in this manner, 'Then Enkidu shall die, but Gilgamesh must not die.'

"And then Shamash, the Sun God, spoke unto valorous Enlil, 'It was by my command that they smote the Bull of Heaven and also Humbaba. Should now Enkidu perish, although innocent?'

"At this, Enlil was enraged and said unto Shamash, 'It is you who are at fault. You did daily visit them, and walked about with them, like a companion.'

"This was my dream, my friend, and, by this dream, am I greatly distressed."

And it came to pass that Enkidu was stricken, and he lay himself upon his bed. The tears flowed down his cheeks like unto rivers. Enkidu was heartsick. He said unto Gilgamesh, "O my brother, dear brother, the Gods will take me from you. With the dead will I abide for all Eternity. I shall cross the threshold of the Netherworld, and never more set mine eyes upon my dear brother."

Enkidu was overcome by a fever and, in his delirium, he said unto the great Door of Cedar, as if it were a man, "O Door of Cedarwood, stupid and insensate, you understand nothing. For you, over the space of twenty leagues, did I seek the finest timber. Then I perceived the most lofty and most magnificent of Cedars. There was no tree to equal yours in all the land. Seventy-two cubits is your height, twenty-four cubits is your width and one cubit is your thickness. Your hinge pole, your ferrules and your pivots are unsurpassed. I created you and carried you unto Nippur and placed you in the sanctuary of the Great God Enlil. Had I but known, O Door of Cedarwood, how you would requite me, and had I but known, O Door of Cedarwood, that this is how you would manifest your gratitude, I would have raised mine axe and cut you down. I would have lashed you unto a raft and floated you down the river to the Temple of Shamash at Ebabbara. I would have set you up in the doorway of the Temple of Shamash, and there would I have placed the great lion-headed eagle God Anzu. This is because Shamash gave ear to my entreaty and, in time of danger, provided me with a weapon. O Door of Cedarwood, I created you and I set you up and now shall I tear you down. May some future King who comes after me despise you and disdain you. May this King place you where men cannot observe you. Let him obliterate my name and inscribe his own name upon you, and then will the curse fall upon him, and not upon me."

And then did Enkidu tear out his hair and rend his garments. When Gilgamesh heard these words of Enkidu, his friend, tears came to his eyes and flowed down his face. And Gilgamesh said unto Enkidu, "My friend, you, who possessed understanding and good sense, do now proclaim all manner of blasphemy. Wherefore, my friend, does your heart utter all manner of sacrilege? Your dream was, in sooth, an important omen, but quite worrisome. This worry has set your lips to buzzing like flies. Though frightening, your dream is a significant portent. You must know the Gods have decreed that the lot of the living is to grieve. Your dream ordains mourning for the one who survives. Now shall I pray unto the Great Gods. Unto Shamash, the Sun God, will I offer words of supplication. I will beseech Anu, Lord of the Gods, on your behalf. Unto Enlil, the Great Counselor, will I beg deliverance for you. And, for you, shall I fashion a statue of gold beyond measure in your likeness. There is no quantity of silver, no quantity of gold, which may erase what Enlil has ordained. What Enlil has ordained cannot be annulled. My friend, it is the Destiny of every man to die. What is unknowable is the hour of his Death."

At the first light of dawn, Enkidu raised his head and cried aloud unto Shamash. Beneath the rays of the Sun, Enkidu wept tears of anguish and said, "O Shamash, I appeal unto you to spare my precious life. And, as to that foul wretch of a hunter who found me naked and unsullied in the wilderness, and thereby did sunder me from a state of Grace, may his traps always be empty and his quarry always elude him. Make his prey always be meager, so that he will lose his livelihood."

And, after he had execrated the hunter to his heart's content, Enkidu did then resolve to curse Shamhat, the temple harlot who had taken his innocence. Enkidu said, "Hear me, Woman. I shall now decree your Fate. Your woes will never end and shall last for all Eternity. I will place the greatest of all curses upon you. Desolation shall overcome you forthwith. Never shall you know the love of a child or the pleasures of a household. Never shall there be satisfaction of your desire. You shall not dwell in the company of women of good breeding. Your finest garments will be bestained by the vomit of drunkards. And your lover will prefer younger and more beauteous girls. He will treat you as a potter treats clay. Objects of beauty will you never acquire, no bright alabaster, no banquet table, heaped high with tasty comestibles, to enjoy. No comfortable featherbed will you sleep upon, but only a crude bench of hardwood. The crossroads shall be your abode. Bare ruined fields will be wherein you slumber. The shadow of a broken wall shall be the place where you ply your trade. Briars and thorns will pierce your bare feet.

Both drunk and sober will strike your cheek. Many will be the verdicts adjudicated against you. The roof of your shelter will leak from the rain, and the builder will not seal the leak thereof. The rabble in the street shall hurl curses and epithets after you as you stroll abroad. The owl will nest above your sleeping-place. And a hearty feast shall never grace your table. You will be stripped of your purple finery and wear only soiled undergarments.

"By reason that you tainted me when I was pure and undefiled in the wilderness do I now cast my curse upon you. Yea, I was pure and undefiled in the wilderness, and there you did seduce and corrupt me."

When Shamash, the Sun God, heard these words of Enkidu, he did call out to him from the Heavens, "O Enkidu, why curse you the temple harlot Shamhat? Bread fit for a God did she feed unto you. Wine fit for a King did she pour for you. She did clothe you in splendid raiment. And, for a comrade, she did give unto you well-favored Gilgamesh. Now shall Gilgamesh, your friend and your brother, grant you to lie down upon a magnificent bed. Gilgamesh will have you rest upon a bed of honor near unto his left hand. And then shall the Princes of the Earth kiss your feet. The dwellers in Uruk will bewail and bemoan and lament your Death. The pleasure-seeking people of Uruk will be overcome with woe. And, after you are dead, Gilgamesh will let his hair grow long and matted, and will don the pelt of a lion, and will wander throughout the length and breadth of the wilderness in mourning."

Enkidu gave ear to the words of glorious Shamash and his wrathful heart was appeased and his fury abated. Enkidu relented and said unto Shamhat, the temple harlot, "Come, Shamhat, I ordain for you a different Destiny. My mouth, which cursed you, shall now bless you instead. Kings, Princes and Nobles shall be smitten with ardor for you. At two leagues remove from you shall a man comb out his locks in anticipation. At one league remove from you shall a man's loins tingle in anticipation. The man who embraces you shall not hesitate to undo his girdle and uncover his treasure. Upon you shall he bestow obsidian, lapis lazuli and gold. Ear bangles and finger rings shall he bestow upon you. Ishtar, Goddess of Love and Fertility, will cause you to know the man whose wealth is bountiful and whose granaries are heaped to overflowing. For you shall this man forsake his wife, though she be the mother of seven of his children."

And, as Enkidu did lie in his sickbed, alone and forlorn, his spirit was troubled and he had a dream. Whereupon it befell that Enkidu did relate his dream unto Gilgamesh thus, "My friend, I have had another dream. In my dream, the Firmament roared and the Earth rendered reply. Between Heaven and Earth did I stand. Then I perceived a man. Dark was his countenance, and fearsome it was. His aspect was like unto the great lion-headed eagle God Anzu. His paws were the paws of a lion. His talons were the talons of an eagle. He grasped me by my hair and prevailed over me. I smote him, but he sprang back like a gate. He struck me and, like unto a raft, overturned me. Upon me, like a mighty wild bull, did he trample. He drenched my body with his slaver. I cried out unto you, Gilgamesh. I cried out, 'Succor me, my friend.' But you answered not. You were affrighted and you did not rescue me. Then the man touched me and mine arms were transformed into the wings of a dove. And then he trussed me up and led me down unto the House of Darkness, the abode of Ereshkigal, Queen of the Netherworld. He led me down unto that dwelling-place from whence none who enters ever returns. Aye, the road wherefrom there can be no returning. Unto the house whose tenants are ever bereft of daylight. There, dust is their sustenance and mud is their food. In that place, feathers are their garments, like unto birds. Yea, there they view no light, but exist in darkness. And, on the door and on the bolt, lies a thick layer of grime.

"Upon all the House of Darkness lay the stillness of Death. When I did enter therein, I perceived the erstwhile Monarchs of the Earth, their crowns fallen to the dirt in humbled heaps. I saw those who once wore regal crowns, who of old reigned over vast lands, who once served roast meat and bread unto the Gods Anu and Enlil, and once poured for them cool water from skins. In the House of Darkness wherein I entered I did behold all manner of Priests, High Priests and Acolytes, Purification Priests and Ecstatic Priests, the Priests who were Anointers of the Great Gods. I beheld Etana, King of Kish, who was carried unto Heaven upon the back of an eagle. I beheld Sumuqan, God of Animals. And there did I behold the Goddess Ereshkigal, Queen of the Netherworld, and before her, squatted Beletseri, Scribe of the Netherworld, reading from the Tablet of Destinies in which every man's Fate is inscribed. Whereupon did the Goddess Ereshkigal raise up her head and espy me and say, 'Who has brought this man hither?'

"I have endured all manner of travail and hardship with you, Gilgamesh. Remember me, my friend, and do not forget all that we have undergone together."

And then did Gilgamesh utter these words unto Enkidu, "My friend, you have had a portentous dream. You must know the Gods have decreed that the lot of the living is to grieve. Your dream ordains mourning for the one who survives. Now shall I pray unto the Great Gods. Unto Shamash, the Sun God, will I offer words of supplication. I will beseech Anu, Lord of the Gods, on your behalf. Unto Enlil, the Great Counselor, will I beg deliverance for you. And, for you, shall I fashion a statue of gold beyond measure in your likeness. There is no quantity of silver, no quantity of gold, which may erase what Enlil has ordained. What Enlil has ordained cannot be annulled. My friend, it is the Destiny of every man to die. What is unknowable is the hour of his Death."

And, on the day Enkidu had his dream, was his strength depleted, and he grew weary. Enkidu lay upon his bed that day and that night. Enkidu lay upon his bed a second day. Enkidu was ill. Enkidu lay upon his bed a third day and a fourth day. Enkidu grew ever more ill. Enkidu lay upon his bed a fifth day and a sixth day. Enkidu lay upon his bed a seventh day and an eighth day and a ninth day and a tenth day. Enkidu's illness grew ever worse. Enkidu lay upon his bed an eleventh day and a twelfth day. And then did Enkidu cry out to Gilgamesh, "My friend, the Gods have cursed me and I die in shame. No glory shall I have, unlike a warrior who falls in battle. I feared combat, so I must die in my bed. The soldier who dies in battle is blessed for his valor. But I shall not fall in battle, and so my name will never attain everlasting renown."

And then did Gilgamesh see Enkidu breathe his last. And Gilgamesh wept for his friend.

Tablet VIII

At the first light of dawn did Gilgamesh utter these words over the body of Enkidu, "O Enkidu, a gazelle was your Dam and a wild ass your Sire. You were reared on the milk of beasts in the wilderness. The wild animals did show you the greenest pasturages. May the paths that led you unto the Forest of Cedars mourn for you all day and all night without cease. May the Elders of high-wall'd Uruk weep for you. May the multitudes of high-wall'd Uruk lament for you. May the hillocks and the mountains mourn for you. May the meadows and fields weep for you as a mother would. May the Cypress tree and the Cedar tree, which we cut down in our rage, bewail you. May the bear grieve for you, and the hyena, panther, tiger, deer, jackal, lion, wild bull, ibex and all manner of wild creatures lament for you.

"May the sacred river Ulaja mourn for you, along whose banks we once walked proudly. May the pure Euphrates weep for you, whose waters we once offered in libation unto the Gods. May the men of high-wall'd Uruk, who bore witness when we slew the Bull of Heaven in glorious combat, grieve for you. May the ploughman bewail you as he sings his harvest lay, when his crops he does bring in. May the masses of the teeming city of Uruk wail for you and exalt your name. May the shepherd in his sheepfold mourn you, who once bestowed upon you milk and butter. May the brewer bewail you, who once gave you beer to quaff. May the harlot who anointed your body with fragrant oils grieve for you. May the joyous wedding guests weep for you. May brothers mourn you as a brother and may sisters mourn you as a brother. And may the tresses of the Lamentation Priests be loosened down their backs like women in mourning. I, myself, as if I were your mother and your father, will mourn for you."

And it befell that Gilgamesh did then address the populace of Uruk and say, "Hearken unto me, O Elders of Uruk. Hearken unto me, O men of Uruk. I mourn for Enkidu, my friend. I weep bitter tears for Enkidu, like those of a wailing woman. He was the battle-axe at my side, in which my hand trusted. The sword in my belt was he. He was the shield which was my protection. He was my festive robes and my most precious jewel. But now has an ill wind arisen and stolen my dearest companion away. And now has sorrow assailed me and cast me down in affliction. O, Enkidu, my friend, who pursued the swift wolf of the mountain, the lion of the plains and the panther of the wilderness. O, Enkidu, my friend, who pursued the swift wolf of the mountain, the lion of the plains and the panther of the wilderness. At my side did you stand as we ascended the mountain. Together we vanquished Humbaba, Guardian of the Forest of Cedar. Together we seized and slaughtered the Bull of Heaven. What is this sleep that has now overcome you? Your visage has become obscure and you hear me not."

But Enkidu did not open his eyes. Gilgamesh touched the heart of Enkidu, but it beat no longer. So Gilgamesh placed a veil over the face of his friend, as one veils a bride. And then Gilgamesh did circle about Enkidu, like unto an eagle. Like a lioness, whose whelps are lost, did Gilgamesh roar, and pace to and fro, back and forth did he pace. And then did Gilgamesh tear out his hair and his beard in anguish. His splendid garments did he rip and rend and cast down, as if they were hateful unto him.

And, at the first light of dawn, Gilgamesh issued a proclamation throughout all the land. Gilgamesh commanded thus, "Hear ye, blacksmith, lapidary, stonecutter, coppersmith, goldsmith. Make, for me, a magnificent statue of my friend, Enkidu. Fashion an image, the like of which has never been seen before. Make his beard of lapis lazuli and his chest of gold. And, about the statue, inlay all manner of precious stones."

And it came to pass that Gilgamesh did then mourn Enkidu for the space of six days and seven nights. For the space of six days and seven nights did Gilgamesh mourn Enkidu, and he would in nowise suffer his friend to be buried, until, at last, a maggot crawled out of his nostril.

Then did Gilgamesh say these words unto Enkidu, "Upon a final resting place of Honor shall I place you, my Friend. I will lay you upon a splendid sepulcher at my left. The Princes of the Earth shall kiss your feet in homage. I will cause all the people of Uruk to lament in your honor. The pleasure-seeking people of Uruk will wail in grief over you. And, after you have gone to your bier, will I allow my hair to become long and matted, and I shall don the skin of a lion and wander in the wilderness."

And, at the first light of dawn, did Gilgamesh arise and enter into the storehouse of treasures. He broke the seal thereof and assayed his riches. Gold, silver, carnelian, obsidian, lapis lazuli and alabaster did he assay. All manner of precious gems artfully worked did Gilgamesh inspect. And then did Gilgamesh provide for his friend, Enkidu, for his journey unto the Netherworld, thirty weights of gold. Also did he provide for his friend thirty weights of ivory. Also did he provide for his friend thirty weights of silver. Also did he provide for his friend thirty weights of iron. He provided for his friend a sword, the handle of which was inlaid with a thickness of gold. He provided for his friend a longbow, which was inlaid with a thickness of gold, and a quiver with fletched arrows of ivory. He provided for his friend a battle-axe, the handle of which held forty weights of gold, and three cubits was its length. And then did Gilgamesh slaughter fattened oxen and sheep, and heap them high for Enkidu, his friend. And this sacrificial meat Gilgamesh did offer unto the Rulers of the Netherworld.

Unto Ishtar, the Great Queen, did Gilgamesh make an offering of a javelin of sacred wood. And Gilgamesh did then say, "May Ishtar, the Great Queen, accept this offering. May she welcome my friend and walk by his side."

Unto Sin, God of the Moon, did Gilgamesh make an offering of an urn of alabaster. And Gilgamesh did then say, "May Sin, God of the Moon, accept this offering. May he welcome my friend and walk by his side."

Unto Ereshkigal, Queen of the Netherworld, did Gilgamesh make an offering of a flagon of lapis lazuli. And Gilgamesh did then say, "May Ereshkigal, Queen of the Netherworld, accept this offering. May she welcome my friend and walk by his side."

Unto Tammuz, the shepherd, beloved consort of Ishtar, did Gilgamesh make an offering of a flute of carnelian. And Gilgamesh did then say, "May Tammuz, the shepherd, beloved consort of Ishtar, accept this offering. May he welcome my friend and walk by his side."

Unto Namtar, Chief Minister of the Netherworld, did Gilgamesh make an offering of a scepter of lapis lazuli and a seat of lapis lazuli. And Gilgamesh did then say, "May Namtar, Chief Minister of the Netherworld, accept this offering. May he welcome my friend and walk by his side."

Unto Hushbisha, Overseer of the Netherworld, did Gilgamesh make an offering of a neck collar of gold and silver, inlaid with carnelian. And Gilgamesh did then say, "May Hushbisha, Overseer of the Netherworld, accept this offering. May she welcome my friend and walk by his side."

Unto Qassatabat, Servant of Ereshkigal, did Gilgamesh make an offering of a bracelet of silver and a ring of gold. And Gilgamesh did then say, "May Qassatabat, Servant of Ereshkigal, accept this offering. May he welcome my friend and walk by his side."

Unto Ninshuluhha, Custodian of the Netherworld, did Gilgamesh make an offering of a vessel of alabaster, the inside of which was inlaid with lapis lazuli and carnelian, and which displayed an image of the Forest of Cedars. And Gilgamesh did then say, "May Ninshuluhha, Custodian of the Netherworld, accept this offering. May she welcome my friend and walk by his side."

Unto Bibbu, Meat Carver of the Netherworld, did Gilgamesh make an offering of a double-edged blade of obsidian with a haft of lapis lazuli bearing an image of the pure Euphrates. And Gilgamesh did then say, "May Bibbu, Meat Carver of the Netherworld, accept this offering. May he welcome my friend and walk by his side."

Unto Dumuziabzu, Scapegoat of the Netherworld, did Gilgamesh make an offering of a coffer of alabaster, inlaid with carnelian, the lid of which was lapis lazuli. And Gilgamesh did then say, "May Dumuziabzu, Scapegoat of the Netherworld, accept this offering. May he welcome my friend and walk by his side, so that Enkidu, my friend, be not heartsick."

And it came to pass that Gilgamesh ordained that a great table of sacred wood be brought forth. Upon this table did he fill a carnelian bowl with honey. Upon this table did he fill a lapis lazuli bowl with cream. Then did Gilgamesh adorn and display these precious bowls, and did offer them up unto Shamash, the Sun God.

Tablet IX

And Gilgamesh wept bitter tears for his friend, Enkidu. Gilgamesh wept bitter tears as he wandered o'er the wilderness. And Gilgamesh cried out in anguish, "Shall I not die also? Shall I not die as Enkidu did? Despair has overcome mine heart. I fear Death as I roam the wilderness. For this reason will I set out on the road to seek immortal Utanapishtim, son of Ubartutu. Unto Utanapishtim did the Gods grant everlasting life after the Great Deluge. I shall journey over these mountain passes in the darkness. If lions I espy and terror assails me, I shall lift up my eyes unto Sin, God of the Moon, and beseech him to succor me."

That night Gilgamesh slept in the mountain fastness, but he did not dream. And so he did awake in anger and perceive a pride of lions before him, rejoicing in life. Gilgamesh took the battle-axe in his hand. He drew his sword from its scabbard. He fell upon the lions like an arrow shot from a bow. Gilgamesh smote the lions, slew them and scattered them. And then did Gilgamesh exult in the slaughter of the beasts.

Gilgamesh clad himself in the pelts of the lions. Gilgamesh ate the flesh of the lions. And then did Gilgamesh dig wells which never ere were there. He drank water from the wells. And then did Gilgamesh pursue the wild winds, but he caught them not.

Because of this was Shamash, the Sun God, troubled. Shamash peered down from the Heavens and said unto Gilgamesh, "O Gilgamesh, wherefore do you rove thus? The everlasting life you seek you shall not find."

And Gilgamesh said unto glorious Shamash, "After my days of restless roaming o'er the wilderness, there shall be ample time for repose in the Netherworld. For all Eternity shall I sleep therein. For now, let mine eyes see the Sun, that I may have my fill of light. In the Netherworld, darkness is endless. Never may the Dead behold the brilliance of Your Majesty, the Sun."

And it came to pass at last that Gilgamesh did arrive at Mashu, the mountain with two peaks. This was the place which does daily guard the rising and setting of Shamash, the Sun God. The peaks of Mashu touch the Vault of Heaven and the base of Mashu reaches down unto the Netherworld. At the portals of Mashu did two Scorpion-sentries stand watch. Terrifying was their aspect, and their very glance was Death. Their fearsome radiance spread over all the mountain, for they kept vigil over the rising and setting of the Sun.

When Gilgamesh espied these creatures, he was overcome with fear and dismay, and he covered his face. But then did Gilgamesh regain his courage and approach them.

When the Scorpion-male beheld Gilgamesh, he did cry out unto his mate, "Lo, he who comes before us, his body is the flesh of Gods."

To which the Scorpion-female made reply thus, "Two-thirds of him is a God, one-third of him is a Man."

And then did the Scorpion-male say unto Gilgamesh, Flesh of the Gods, "Who are you, who have travelled so distant a journey? How came you to be in my presence? How did you traverse so many arduous and perilous mountains, rivers and seas unto this land which, hitherto, no man's eyes have seen? The purpose of your voyage I desire to know."

Gilgamesh spoke thus, "I am called Gilgamesh. I seek Utanapishtim, my forebear, who took his place in the Assembly of the Gods, and was granted life everlasting. Of Death and Eternal Life I wish to learn the secret."

The Scorpion-male said unto Gilgamesh, "No man born of woman, O Gilgamesh, has ever made that passage. Never has a mortal accomplished that feat. No one has travelled the distant and rigorous path through the innards of the mountain. The crossing is by means of the Road of the Sun for the space of twelve hours. Therein is no light, but only utter darkness. Through the innards of the mountain does the Sun journey when it is night. From thence does the Sun exit when it is Dawn and return thereunto when it is Dusk. And you, Gilgamesh, how mean you to achieve this undertaking?"

At this, the Scorpion-female spoke these words, "Gilgamesh has distress in his breast. Torment and ache has he suffered. His face is weathered by cold and heat. Though exhausted, he must go on. Now, therefore, open the Gate of the Mountain for Gilgamesh."

Whereupon did the Scorpion-male say unto Gilgamesh, Flesh of the Gods, "Go, Gilgamesh. Enter into the Mountain of Mashu. May your feet carry you forward in safety. For you is the Gate of the Mountain open."

When Gilgamesh gave ear to these words of the Scorpion-male, he did heed them and swiftly set out upon the Road of the Sun. Gilgamesh ran through the mountain for one hour. All was darkness, and light there was none. Gilgamesh could in nowise see before him nor behind him. Neither could he see to either side of him.

Gilgamesh ran through the mountain for two hours. All was darkness, and light there was none. Gilgamesh could in nowise see before him nor behind him. Neither could he see to either side of him.

Gilgamesh ran through the mountain for three hours. All was darkness, and light there was none. Gilgamesh could in nowise see before him nor behind him. Neither could he see to either side of him.

Gilgamesh ran through the mountain for four hours. All was darkness, and light there was none. Gilgamesh could in nowise see before him nor behind him. Neither could he see to either side of him.

Gilgamesh ran through the mountain for five hours. All was darkness, and light there was none. Gilgamesh could in nowise see before him nor behind him. Neither could he see to either side of him.

Gilgamesh ran through the mountain for six hours. All was darkness, and light there was none. Gilgamesh could in nowise see before him nor behind him. Neither could he see to either side of him.

Gilgamesh ran through the mountain for seven hours. All was darkness, and light there was none. Gilgamesh could in nowise see before him nor behind him. Neither could he see to either side of him.

Gilgamesh ran through the mountain for eight hours. Then it was that Gilgamesh cried out in pain and anguish. All was darkness, and light there was none. Gilgamesh could in nowise see before him nor behind him. Neither could he see to either side of him.

Gilgamesh ran through the mountain for nine hours. Then it was that Gilgamesh felt the North Wind upon his face, and it did chill him. All was darkness, and light there was none. Gilgamesh could in nowise see before him nor behind him. Neither could he see to either side of him.

When Gilgamesh had run for ten hours, the time for the rising of the Sun drew nearer.

When Gilgamesh had run for eleven hours, just one hour of running remained for him before the emergence of the Sun. And, then, at the end of the twelfth hour, did Gilgamesh come out from within the mountain, just in advance of the course of the Sun. And then did Gilgamesh behold the brilliance of Shamash, the Sun God, in all his glory.

And it came to pass that Gilgamesh then espied before him the Garden of the Gods. Precious gems hung from the branches of the trees in the Garden. One tree bore fruit of carnelian, hanging therefrom like bunches of grapes. This tree was pleasing to the sight. Another tree bore leaves of lapis lazuli in full bloom. This tree was a delight to behold. There were trees bejeweled with fruit of ruby, diamond, emerald, agate, sapphire, citrine, hematite, and also were there pearls and coral from the sea. And Gilgamesh gazed in awe at the beauty and magnificence of the Garden of the Gods.

And then did Shamash, the Sun God, take pity upon Gilgamesh. Shamash saw that Gilgamesh was clad in the pelts of lions and had partaken of the flesh of lions. Shamash was touched by the plight of Gilgamesh, and he spoke unto him thus, "O Gilgamesh, never has a mortal crossed this way before. And never shall one, so long as the gales drive the waters. Why do you run this way, forasmuch as the eternal life which you seek you shall not find?"

Whereat Gilgamesh did make reply unto glorious Shamash in this manner, "Shall I, after I have roamed hither and thither across the expanse of the wilderness as a wanderer, lay my head down within the bowels of the Earth, and slumber throughout the years forever and ever? Let mine eyes behold the Sun, and be sated with the light. Yea, let the darkness be banished, if only for a brief moment. For when shall the man who is dead ever gaze upon the light of the Sun?"

Tablet X

Beyond the Garden of the Gods, beside the shore of the sea, dwelt Siduri, the Maker of Wine. She sat upon a stool, her golden vat of fermenting grapes at her side. Upon her face a veil she wore. Gilgamesh perceived her and did approach her. He was clad in the pelts of lions, and fearsome was his aspect. Gilgamesh was made of the flesh of Gods, but woe did he bear in his breast. And his countenance was like unto one who has travelled upon a wearisome journey.

Siduri, the Maker of Wine, looked in the distance and beheld Gilgamesh draw near unto her. Whereupon did Siduri say to herself, "Surely, this is one who would bring harm to a woman. Whither does he advance?"

Scarce had Siduri seen Gilgamesh when she did run into her house. She barred the door thereof and locked the bolt and ascended unto the roof. But Gilgamesh heard the shot of the bolt of the door forcibly shut. And then did Gilgamesh stand before the door of the house and look up at Siduri and exclaim, "Maker of Wine, wherefore did you bolt your door when you perceived me? Your door will I smash down. Your bolt will I break asunder."

And Siduri made reply unto Gilgamesh thus, "I was apprehensive because your appearance frightened me so. I barred the door of my house and locked the bolt and fled unto the roof. Be so kind as to inform me of your name and your intention."

Gilgamesh said unto Siduri, the Maker of Wine, "I am Gilgamesh, King of high-wall'd Uruk, who vanquished Humbaba, Guardian of the Forest of Cedars. I am Gilgamesh, King of high-wall'd Uruk, who seized and slaughtered the Bull of Heaven. I am Gilgamesh, King of high-wall'd Uruk, who put to rout and smote lions in the mountain passes."

At this did Siduri, the Maker of Wine, say unto Gilgamesh, "If you indeed be Gilgamesh, King of high-wall'd Uruk, who vanquished Humbaba, Guardian of the Forest of Cedars, who seized and slaughtered the Bull of Heaven, and who put to rout and smote lions in the mountain passes, wherefore is your vigor so wasted and your cheeks so sunken? Wherefore is your face so wretched and why is your spirit so sorrowful? Why resemble you like unto one who has undertaken a long and arduous journey? Why is your countenance weathered by cold and by heat? And why do you wander the wilderness clad in lion skins in pursuit of the wind?"

Gilgamesh made reply unto Siduri, the Maker of Wine, thus, "Wherefore should not my vigor be wasted and my cheeks so sunken? Should not my face appear wretched and my spirit sorrowful? Should I not resemble one who has undertaken a long and arduous journey? Should not my countenance be weathered by cold and by heat? And should I not wander the wilderness clad in lion skins in pursuit of the wind? My friend, Enkidu, my comrade, who hunted the swift wild stallion of the hills and the panther of the plains, has met the Fate of all mankind. We together overcame all manner of hardship and travail, and ascended the mountain. Together we vanquished and killed Humbaba, Guardian of the Forest of Cedars, and together we seized and slew the Bull of Heaven. But then did untimely Death take him from me. So I did mourn him for the space of six days and seven nights, and did not consign him to the tomb until a maggot crawled out of his nostril.

"And then did the fear of Death overcome me. For this reason do I rove o'er the wilderness and find no comfort or repose. The issue of my friend's demise weighs heavily upon me and oppresses me. How can I remain silent? How can I not give voice to my grief? He whom I loved has become unto dust. Enkidu, my friend, has perished and become unto dust. Shall I not also lay me down like Enkidu, never to arise again for all Eternity? O, Maker of Wine, now that I, at last, look upon your visage, let me not see the face of Death, that which I fear so much."

At this did Siduri, the Maker of Wine, say unto Gilgamesh, "Gilgamesh, wherefore do you wander so? Never will you find the eternal life you seek. For the Gods, when first they created mortals, allotted Death unto mankind, but life everlasting the Gods retained in their keeping. As for you, Gilgamesh, let your stomach always be full. Be of good cheer each day and each night. Fill each day with merriment. With dancing and rejoicing let every day be abounding. Fresh and clean should be your raiment. Aye, let your hair be clean washed. Bathe yourself in pure water. Cherish the little child who holds your hand. Bring joy to the loins of your wife. This, then, is the work of man."

But Gilgamesh made reply thus unto Siduri, the Maker of Wine, "What say you, Maker of Wine? Heartsick am I for my friend. Now relate unto me which is the way to Utanapishtim. Vouchsafe unto me its markers. Tell them to me, and directions withal. If it be possible, even the Ocean itself will I traverse. But, if it should be impossible, then I shall roam further o'er the wilderness."

Thus did Siduri, the Maker of Wine, say unto Gilgamesh, "O Gilgamesh, never has there been such a crossing. From days of yore, has no man been able to traverse the Ocean. Only valorous Shamash, the Sun God, does cross the Ocean. Save for Shamash, who could make such a perilous crossing? The voyage is dangerous, and treacherous is the course. Aye, and midway lie the Waters of Death, which are deep and which bar the approaches. The mere touch of a drop of the Waters of Death is instant demise. So, Gilgamesh, if perchance you succeed in traversing the Ocean, what will you do when you arrive at the Waters of Death?

"Yet there is one who may, peradventure, assist you in your quest. He is called Urshanabi, the Ferryman of Utanapishtim. You shall find him in the depths of the forest felling pine trees. The Beings of Stone, who are not harmed by the Waters of Death, are with him. Let him behold your countenance. And, if it be possible, cross the Ocean with him. But, if not, then you must retrace your steps back to whence you came."

When Gilgamesh gave ear to these words, he put hand to axe and drew the dagger from his belt. He entered the forest and crept stealthily forward until he espied the Beings of Stone. Then, like unto an arrow, did Gilgamesh fall upon them. In the depths of the forest did the battle cry of Gilgamesh resound. Urshanabi saw the flash of Gilgamesh's dagger and raised his own axe to strike. But Gilgamesh struck first. Gilgamesh smote the head of Urshanabi with the side of his axe. Then did Gilgamesh seize Urshanabi's arms and press down upon his chest. Urshanabi was defeated. And then did the Beings of Stone, without whom no one crosses, take fright. Gilgamesh stayed not his hand. He shattered the Beings of Stone and hurled them into the river. The Beings of Stone sank beneath the waters.

Then did Gilgamesh turn back and stand before Urshanabi. Whereupon did Urshanabi cast his eye upon Gilgamesh and say, "Prithee, tell me how you are called. I am called Urshanabi, the Ferryman of Utanapishtim, the Distant One."

Gilgamesh made reply unto Urshanabi thus, "I am Gilgamesh, King of high-wall'd Uruk. I am come hither from Uruk, the abode of Anu. I have crossed the high mountains. I have traversed the Road of the Sun through the innards of the mountain Mashu. Now that I behold your visage, Urshanabi, show me the way unto Utanapishtim, the Distant One."

And Urshanabi said unto Gilgamesh, "Wherefore is your vigor so wasted and your cheeks so sunken? Wherefore is your face so wretched and why is your spirit so sorrowful? Why resemble you like unto one who has undertaken a long and arduous journey? Why is your countenance weathered by cold and by heat? And why do you wander the wilderness clad in lion skins in pursuit of the wind?"

Gilgamesh made reply unto Urshanabi, the Ferryman of Utanapishtim, thus, "Should not my vigor be wasted and my cheeks so sunken? Should not my face appear wretched and my spirit sorrowful? Should I not resemble one who has undertaken a long and arduous journey? Should not my countenance be weathered by cold and by heat? And should I not wander the wilderness clad in lion skins in pursuit of the wind? My friend, Enkidu, my comrade, who hunted the swift wild stallion of the hills and the panther of the plains, has met the Fate of all mankind. We together overcame all manner of hardship and travail, and ascended the mountain. Together we vanquished and killed Humbaba, Guardian of the Forest of Cedars, and together we seized and slew the Bull of Heaven. But then did untimely

Death take him from me. So I did mourn him for the space of six days and seven nights, and did not consign him to the tomb until a maggot crawled out of his nostril.

"And then did the fear of Death overcome me. For this reason do I rove o'er the wilderness and find no comfort or repose. The issue of my friend's demise weighs heavily upon me and oppresses me. How can I remain silent? How can I not give voice to my grief? He whom I loved has become unto dust. Enkidu, my friend, has perished and become unto dust. Shall I not also lay me down like Enkidu, never to arise again for all Eternity? Therefore, Urshanabi, relate unto me which is the way to Utanapishtim. Vouchsafe unto me its markers. Tell them to me, and directions withal. If it be possible, even the Ocean itself will I traverse. But, if it should be impossible, then I shall roam further o'er the wilderness."

Then did Urshanabi say unto Gilgamesh, "Your own hand has indeed hindered the crossing you wish for. When you shattered the Beings of Stone and hurled them into the river, you did forfeit any chance of transiting the Ocean. The Beings of Stone were not harmed by the Waters of Death. They carried me over the water and, by this means, did they allow me to cross in safety and unharmed. But now, Gilgamesh, there remains only one other way. Take your axe to hand and go into the forest. Cut you three hundred rods. Cut them sixty cubits in length and coat them with pitch. Into each rod carve a socket. And bring these rods unto me."

When Gilgamesh heard these words, took he the axe in his hand and the dagger from his belt. He went into the forest and cut three hundred rods. He cut them sixty cubits in length and did coat them with pitch. Into each rod did he carve a socket. And then did he carry the rods unto Urshanabi, the Ferryman.

Whereupon did Gilgamesh and Urshanabi launch the boat. Together, did Gilgamesh and Urshanabi embark upon their voyage. On the third day they had travelled the distance of a journey of a month and a half. Now had they arrived at the Waters of Death.

And then did Urshanabi say unto Gilgamesh, "Let not your hand touch the Waters of Death, lest you perish. Take a rod and thrust us forward, but do not use that rod another time. Instead, discard the rod and take up a second one. Then, Gilgamesh, take up a third rod, and a fourth, and a fifth. Then, Gilgamesh, take up a sixth rod, and a seventh, and an eighth. Then, Gilgamesh, take up a ninth rod, and a tenth, and an eleventh, and a twelfth rod, and heave us forward."

When Gilgamesh had used three hundred rods, he ceased his labors. Then did Gilgamesh undo his sash and remove his garment. And then did Gilgamesh hold high his garment, that it should serve as a sail.

From the shore did Utanapishtim behold Gilgamesh approach at a distance. And Utanapishtim spoke unto himself in this manner, "Wherefore have the Beings of Stone, who are the crew of that boat, been destroyed? Aye, and why is another beside the master embarked thereon? He who comes hither is no man of mine. I look at him, but he is no man of mine."

Then did the boat make land upon the strand of the shore. Whereupon did Gilgamesh disembark and draw near unto Utanapishtim. And then did Gilgamesh say to Utanapishtim, "Old man, I seek Utanapishtim, the Distant One. After the Great Deluge, Utanapishtim, my forebear, took his place in the Assembly of the Gods, and was granted life everlasting. Of Death and Eternal Life I wish to learn the secret."

And Utanapishtim said unto Gilgamesh, "Wherefore is your vigor so wasted and your cheeks so sunken? Wherefore is your face so wretched and why is your spirit so sorrowful? Why resemble you like unto one who has undertaken a long and arduous journey? Why is your countenance weathered by cold and by heat? And why do you wander the wilderness clad in lion skins in pursuit of the wind?"

Gilgamesh made reply unto Utanapishtim, the Distant One, thus, "Should not my vigor be wasted and my cheeks so sunken? Should not my face appear wretched and my spirit sorrowful? Should I not resemble one who has undertaken a long and arduous journey? Should not my countenance be weathered by cold and by heat? And should I not wander the wilderness clad in lion skins in pursuit of the wind? My friend, Enkidu, my comrade, who hunted the swift wild stallion of the hills and the panther of the plains, has met the Fate of all mankind. We together overcame all manner of hardship and travail, and ascended the mountain. Together we vanquished and killed Humbaba, Guardian of the Forest of Cedars, and together we seized and slew the Bull of Heaven. But then did untimely Death take him from me. So I did mourn him for the space of six days and seven nights, and did not consign him to the tomb until a maggot crawled out of his nostril.

"And then did the fear of Death overcome me. For this reason do I rove o'er the wilderness and find no comfort or repose. The issue of my friend's demise weighs heavily upon me and oppresses me. How can I remain silent? How can I not give voice to my grief? He whom I loved has become unto dust. Enkidu, my friend, has perished and become unto dust. Shall I not also lay me down like Enkidu, never to arise again for all Eternity?

"That was when I bethought myself to journey afield to find Utanapishtim, the Distant One, of whom men speak. I have traversed many arduous mountains, rivers, deserts and seas. I am weary with traveling and fain would lie down. Sweet slumber has not comforted my body. With sleeplessness am I worn down. My sinews ache from sorrow and grief. And what have I gained from all my efforts? Ere I arrived at the dwelling of the Maker of Wine were my garments spent. I killed bear, hyena, lion, panther, tiger, stag, ibex, all the beasts of the wilderness. Their flesh did I eat and their pelts did I wear. And what have I gained from all my efforts? Let the Gate of Sadness be bolted 'gainst me. Let the door thereof be sealed with tar and pitch. For me shall there be no more dancing, no more music of the harp, no more pleasure of the song. For me is happiness and contentment departed for all time. The most unfortunate and disconsolate of beings am I."

At this did Utanapishtim say unto Gilgamesh, "Why, O Gilgamesh, are you so wretched? Such self-pity is unseemly. You were formed from the flesh of Gods and men. The Gods did favor you as if they were your fathers and mothers. Have you ever, O Gilgamesh, compared your lot with that of a fool? For you did the Gods set a throne in the Assembly and suffer you to rule. The fool is given remainders of unfermented yeast in the stead of butter, coarse bran and offal in the stead of fine bread. The fool wears sackcloth in the stead of splendid apparel. In the stead of a magnificent sash does he wear an old rope. Since no advisors counsel him, he knows not what to do. Think on the fool, O Gilgamesh, and compare your lot to his.

"True it is that the Gods took Enkidu, your friend. But you, O Gilgamesh, you strove without cease, and what did you accomplish? With toil and strife did you wear yourself out. Your sinews and your muscles are tormented with pain. All this does but hasten the onset of the end of your days. The life of a man is as easily broken as a reed in a thicket of cane. Death all too soon cuts down, in their prime, the handsome youth and the comely maiden. No one beholds the face of Death. No one hears the voice of Death. But pitiless and unyielding Death cuts down all. Everything is impermanent. Yet a house we build to stand for all time. Yet a seal we set to a contract for all time. Yet brothers divide a bequest for all time. We yearn for peace, yet hatred and strife there is always in the realm. Ever will the rivers rise and flood the land. We are like unto the Mayfly floating on the waters, gazing upon the Sun, and then we are no more. All is transitory. The sleeping and the dead, how alike they are. They both portray the image of Mortality. No distinction is there between master and servant when both have reached the end of their allotted life span and breathed their last. The Anunnaki, the Assembly of Great Gods, together with Mammetum, Maker of Destiny, do ordain the Fate of men. Both Death and Life do they allot, but the hour of his Death is not for a man to know."

Tablet XI

Gilgamesh said unto Utanapishtim, The Distant One, "I gaze upon you, old man, and now do I know you. You are Utanapishtim, the Distant One, whom I have journeyed so far to seek. But your appearance is in no wise different from mine. In sooth, you look just like me. I was resolved to do battle against you and overcome you and learn your secret. Yet now does some force stay my hand. O tell me, Utanapishtim, how was it that you came to stand in the Assembly of Gods and attain life everlasting?"

And Utanapishtim did make reply unto Gilgamesh in this manner, "I will discover unto you, O Gilgamesh, the whole hidden story. Unto you will I reveal the Secret and the Mystery. Unto you will I reveal the Secret of the Gods. The city of Shuruppak, a place you have knowledge of, is set upon the banks of the river Euphrates. This aforementioned city is ancient, and Gods once dwelled therein. But, in those days of yore, the multitudes teemed upon the face of the Earth and the unceasing clamor and wickedness of the people aroused the wrath of the Gods. And thus the Great Gods purposed a mighty Deluge to rain down in order to wipe out mankind. A vow of secrecy was sworn by the Great Gods. Their father, Anu, Lord of the Gods, swore the oath. Also did their advisor, the valorous Enlil, God of Storms, swear to it. Also did their Chamberlain Ninurta, God of War, swear to it. Also did Ennugi, God of Canals, swear to it.

"Ea, God of Wisdom, the cunning one, did also swear the oath not to relate the secret unto any man. But Ea was crafty. Unto no man did Ea divulge the secret. Instead, Ea spoke the secret unto the reed fence of my house, and I did chance to overhear his words. 'O reed fence, O reed fence, hearken unto my words,' said Ea. 'Pay heed, O reed fence, pay heed to my words. Tell your master, Utanapishtim of Shuruppak, son of Ubaratutu, to pull down his house and fashion a vessel therefrom. Advise him to abandon all possessions and save his life. Tell him to disdain worldly riches and preserve life instead. Aboard this vessel shall he take the seed of every creature that lives upon the Earth. This boat, which he is to build, the measurements shall be equal for the width and the length thereof. Tell him to cover this vessel, as the Firmament covers the Abyss.'

"I apprehended these words of Ea. And I spoke thus unto Ea, my Lord, 'What you have commanded me to do, I shall honor and perform with all diligence. But what shall I reply unto the city of Shuruppak, the populace and the Elders, when they ask of me the reason I build such a boat?'

"And Ea said unto me, his servant, 'You may speak to them in this wise, "Enlil, God of Storms, is wrathful toward me. Therefore I cannot abide in your city. Neither can I set foot upon land which is Enlil's. So I shall descend unto the Deep, there to dwell with Ea, my Lord. But have no concern. Upon you will Enlil, God of Storms, shower great abundance. Yea, a profusion of water-fowl, a myriad of fishes and all manner of sea creatures. A harvest of watery riches will he rain down upon you. At the dawning will he shower a bountiful torrent upon you."' '

"At the first light of dawn, the populace assembled about me. The carpenter carried his axe. The reed-cutter carried his sharpened stone. The blacksmith carried his anvil. The rope-maker carried his cordage. The young men brought pitch. The wealthy brought all that was needful, while the poor brought what they could. I planned the structure of the vessel and drew her design. By the end of the fifth day, the hull was complete. One acre was the expanse of her deck. One hundred and twenty cubits was the height of her sides. I gave her six decks, thus making seven levels in all. The inside of her I divided into nine parts. Then caulking did I put where necessary. The punting poles to propel us did I bring within, and also requisite supplies and provisions. Ten thousand measures of pitch did I pour into the furnace. And ten thousand measures of tar did I employ to smear upon the insides of the vessel. The basket-bearers brought aboard ten thousand measures of oil, in addition to the great quantity of oil which was consumed, and the seven thousand measures of oil which the boatman did stow away.

"Day after day did I slaughter bullocks for the workmen, and also sheep. I gave unto my workmen mead, beer, ale and wine, which they did quaff as if it were water from the river. Each day was a great feast like unto the celebration of the New Year Festival. And then, at last, was the boat finished. At the rising of the Sun, I did anoint and bless the boat with mine own hand. And then, at the setting of the Sun, was she ready to be launched.

"Arduous was the launch. With difficulty did we roll the boat forward upon logs, until two-thirds thereof had entered the water. All that I possessed I laded aboard her. All that I possessed of silver I laded aboard her. All that I possessed of gold I laded aboard her. All that I possessed of the seed of living creatures I laded aboard her. And then did I embark onto the boat all my kindred and family. And then did I embark onto the boat all the animals of the fields and all the beasts of the wild. And then did I embark onto the boat all manner of skilled craftsmen.

"Then Shamash, the Sun God, decreed the hour of the Great Flood, and he said, 'At the dawning, a plenteous rainfall shall pour down. Do now enter into your vessel and bolt fast your hatchway.'

"The appointed time had arrived. I beheld the aspect of the storm, and it was fearsome to me. Therefore did I enter into the vessel and seal shut the hatchway.

Unto Puzuramurri, the shipwright, who sealed the boat, did I bestow what remained of my dwelling, together with all it contained.

"Then, at the first light of dawn, a darkling cloud arose over the horizon. Thundering within this black cloud was Adad, the Storm God. Rushing before this cloud were Shullat, God of Despoilment, and Hanish, God of Destruction, coming as heralds of Doom over mountains and plains. Errakal, God of Plagues, wrenched loose the mooring posts of the world. Ninurta, God of War, made the dikes overflow and unleashed havoc upon the realm. And the Anunnaki, the Assembly of Great Gods, did brandish high their torches and scorch the land with their flames. Desolation was abroad upon the face of the Earth. Then all was stillness as Adad, the Storm God, transformed what was daylight into darkness. And, then, Adad raged and snorted and pawed the ground and charged forward like unto a wild bull and smashed the Earth into pieces as if it were a cauldron of clay.

"For the space of one whole day did the tempest winds rage. The fury of the gale winds blew fierce and hard. And then came the Great Flood. Like a mighty invading army did the waters overwhelm the people. A brother could not discern his own brother, nor could men be espied in the torrent. Even the Gods were stricken with terror by the Great Deluge. They fled and ascended unto the highest Heaven, the Firmament of Anu, Lord of the Gods. And there the Gods did cower like curs, crouching and whimpering beside the walls of the Palace of Anu.

"Then did the Great Goddess Aruru, Mother of All Birth, she of the sweet voice, cry aloud like a woman in childbirth, 'Would that the day had never befallen, when I did propose evil in the Assembly of the Gods. How could I have urged evil in the Assembly of the Gods when I wished for a catastrophe to annihilate my children? Forsooth, have I not given birth to these, my children? Now, like the spawn of fish, do they glut the sea.' And then did the Great Gods, the Anunnaki, weep bitter tears with her. The Great Gods sat with Aruru and cried, humbled and tearful. And the Great Gods suffered hunger and thirst, for mortals no longer offered up food and drink as sacrifice unto the Gods.

"Six days and seven nights did the storm winds blow, the tempest roar and the deluge rain down. The stormflood overwhelmed the land. But, upon the seventh day, the winds did grow calm and the floodwaters did subside, like unto a mighty invading army withdrawing from battle. I peered out upon the face of the Earth. And, lo, all was still. All of humanity was returned unto dust. The surface of the Earth which I could espy was flat as a roof. A hatchway did I open, whereupon sunlight fell upon my cheek. At this, I did fall to my knees and weep. Tears flowed down my face.

"In vain did I search for a landing place on the horizon. To the edge of the world did I look, but of land there was none. Then, at last, at twelve leagues distance, I espied land, and there did the boat run aground. Upon the Mountain of

Nimush did the boat come to rest. The Mountain of Nimush held the boat fast and would not allow it to move. One day and a second day, the Mountain of Nimush held the boat fast and would not allow it to move. A third day and a fourth day, the Mountain of Nimush held the boat fast and would not allow it to move. A fifth day and a sixth day, the Mountain of Nimush held the boat fast and would not allow it to move. Then, when the seventh day dawned, I sent forth a dove and released her. But, to and fro went the dove, and she returned, for a resting place was not to be found. Then a swallow I sent forth and released. But, to and fro went the swallow, and she returned, for a resting place was not to be found. Then a raven I sent forth and released. The raven flew off and saw that the flood waters had abated. Whereupon did the raven eat and caw and preen, and did not return unto me.

"Then did I sacrifice a sheep unto the Four Winds of Heaven. Unto the Gods did I make an offering, and burned incense upon the summit of the mountain. Twice seven flagons did I array as a libation, and also burned fragrant cane, cedar and myrtle. Whereupon did the Gods smell the sweet savor. Aye, the Gods smelt the sweet fragrance and hovered like flies about the sacrifice, for the Gods were hungry.

"And then the Great Goddess Aruru, Mother of All Birth, did arrive. She raised on high the necklace of lapis lazuli which Anu, Lord of the Gods, had bestowed upon her as a love-token. Aruru said these words, 'O you Gods, let this sacred necklace serve as a remembrance of these malevolent days. May I ever be mindful of these days, and never forget them. Let the Gods now approach the sacrificial offering, all save Enlil, God of Storms. Enlil, alone of all the Gods, shall not partake of the offering, for he, unreasoning, occasioned the Great Deluge and, thereby, consigned my children to annihilation.'

"But, then, did Enlil, God of Storms, come thither. When Enlil beheld the boat, he was wrathful. Enlil was swollen with rage against the Gods. Said Enlil, 'How is it that this mortal did survive? No man was to escape the floodwaters of destruction.'

"Ninurta, God of War, made reply thus unto intrepid Enlil, 'Who but Ea, God of Wisdom, could contrive such a stratagem to save mankind? Ea, the cunning one, knows of every artifice.'

"Whereat did Ea say unto valiant Enlil, 'You, O undaunted one, are the wisest of the Gods. How could you, so injudiciously, bring down the Great Deluge to destroy mankind? Aye, chastise the sinner for his sin. Punish the transgressor for his transgression. But have mercy upon he who transgresses not, upon he who sins not. In the stead of a Great Flood, let a lion come forth to devour the sinners. In the stead of a Great Flood, let a wolf come forth to devour the sinners. In the stead of a Great Flood, let a famine be upon the land to strike down the sinners. In the stead of a Great Flood, let a pestilence be upon the land to strike down the sinners. In sooth, I revealed not the secret of the Gods unto any man. I vouchsafed the secret unto a reed fence, and Utanapishtim did chance to overhear me. Now must you deliberate and take counsel as to what the Fate of Utanapishtim shall be.'

"Then did Enlil approach the boat. Mine hand did he take hold of. He commanded me to kneel before him. Then he did grasp the hand of my wife and command her to kneel beside me. Our foreheads he touched as he stood between us, and then did Enlil, God of Storms, bless us. Enlil said, 'Hitherto has Utanapishtim been mortal. Now, from henceforth, shall Utanapishtim, and also his wife, be equal like unto us Gods, and enjoy eternal life. Utanapishtim and his wife shall dwell apart from mortals, afar in the distance, at the source of the rivers.' Thus it befell that the Gods carried me hither and settled me in this place, from whence the rivers flow forth.

"But, as for you, O Gilgamesh, who will convene the Gods on your behalf? Who will speak for you, that you may obtain life everlasting which you seek? Come now, let us ascertain if you are worthy and put you to the test. Let us see if you may remain awake and forsake sleep for six days and seven nights."

And it came to pass that, no sooner had Gilgamesh sat upon his haunches, sleep like a mist swirled over him. Whereupon did Utanapishtim say unto his wife, "O, behold the man who sought eternal life. He has not been able to remain awake and forsake sleep for six days and seven nights. Sleep has swirled over him like a mist."

And his wife said unto Utanapishtim, the Distant One, "Touch Gilgamesh that he may awaken. Let him betake himself homeward in peace upon the road he has traversed."

Utanapishtim made reply to his wife thus, "All men are duplicitous. Even you will he endeavor to deceive. Gilgamesh will affirm that he has slumbered but a wink. Therefore, woman, bake you a loaf of daily bread. Each day bake you a loaf of daily bread. Place each loaf by the head of sleeping Gilgamesh and, on the house-wall, make a mark thereupon for each day that he slumbers."

The wife of Utanapishtim did as she was bidden. She baked a loaf of bread every day and set it beside the head of sleeping Gilgamesh and made a mark upon the house-wall for each day. And the first loaf became hard. The second loaf became like leather. The third loaf became soggy. The fourth loaf became white. The fifth loaf became moldy. The sixth loaf was fresh. The seventh loaf was yet on the embers when Utanapishtim touched Gilgamesh, who awoke from his slumbers.

Whereupon did Gilgamesh say unto Utanapishtim, the Distant One, "Scarce had I closed mine eyes when you did straightaway touch me and rouse me from slumber."

But Utanapishtim said unto Gilgamesh, "Behold, O Gilgamesh, these loaves of bread and number them. This is the count of days you have slept, that the number may be known to you. The first loaf is hard. The second loaf is like leather. The third loaf is soggy. The fourth loaf is white. The fifth loaf is moldy. The sixth loaf is fresh. The seventh loaf was yet on the embers when I did touch you and awaken you from your slumbers."

Gilgamesh said unto Utanapishtim, "What then shall I do, O Utanapishtim, whither shall I go? Death has seized hold of my flesh. He broods in my bedchamber. And, wheresoever I turn, I spy only the face of Death."

And it came to pass that Utanapishtim said unto Urshanabi, the Ferryman, "Woe is unto you, Urshanabi. May the harbor no longer afford you safe haven. May the crossing of the Ocean be hateful unto you. Hereby are you banished from these shores. This man whom you have guided hither, his body reeks with foulness, and animal pelts hide his grace and beauty. Take him from hence, Urshanabi, and lead him unto the place where he may bathe. There shall he lave himself, and wash off his foulness in the pure waters until he be cleansed. There shall he cast off his pelts, that the Sea may carry them away. And let him be anointed with fragrant unguents, so the comeliness of his body is revealed. Grant unto him a new headband, so that his hair shall appear resplendent. Have him don apparel befitting nobility, royal raiment suitable for a King. Until Gilgamesh returns home unto his city and his journey is done, his robes shall betray no sign of age or wear, but will remain ever unsullied and new."

Whereupon did Urshanabi, the Ferryman, lead Gilgamesh unto the washing-place, and did wash his matted hair until it was cleansed. Then Urshanabi cast off the pelts from the body of Gilgamesh, and let the Sea carry them away. Urshanabi anointed Gilgamesh with fragrant unguents. And the comeliness of Gilgamesh's body was revealed. Urshanabi bound Gilgamesh's head with a new headband, so his hair appeared resplendent. Gilgamesh donned apparel befitting nobility, royal raiment suitable for a King. These robes would betray no sign of age or wear, but would remain ever unsullied and new, until Gilgamesh did return home unto his city and his journey was done.

And it came to pass that Gilgamesh and Urshanabi embarked into their vessel. They boarded the boat and launched it upon the billows. Whereupon, the wife of Utanapishtim, the Distant One, said unto her husband, "Came Gilgamesh hither weary and heartsick. What will you now bestow upon him, that he may take with him unto his homeland?"

At this, Gilgamesh did employ his pole to thrust the boat close unto the shore. And Utanapishtim said to Gilgamesh, "Hither did you come, O Gilgamesh, weary and heartsick. What should I now bestow upon you, that you may take with you unto your homeland? I shall reveal unto you, O Gilgamesh, a Secret. It is a hidden Mystery of the Gods. There be a plant very much like a thorn-bush which grows deep under the Ocean. Like a rose, this plant has sharp thorns which will prick you. Yet, if your hand can procure this plant, you shall surely attain life everlasting."

Upon hearing this, Gilgamesh dug a shaft deep into the ground until the Abyss he did reach. He bound heavy stones to his feet, and the stones dragged him down unto the depths of the Sea-bed. There he did espy the plant. As he seized the plant, its thorns did scratch him. Then he did cut loose the heavy stones from his feet, and the Sea carried him upward and cast him upon the shore.

And Gilgamesh said unto Urshanabi, the Ferryman, "Behold this plant, Urshanabi. It is a plant of great wonder. With it, a man may regain his youthful vigor. Unto high-wall'd Uruk shall I carry it. There will I give it unto the Elders to eat in order to test its properties. The name of this plant shall be 'Old man becomes young man.' Then will I eat the plant, that I may once again come to be a youth."

Whereupon did Gilgamesh and Urshanabi set forth upon their journey. After twenty leagues they broke bread. After thirty leagues they rested for the night. And Gilgamesh perceived there a pond of cool water. He descended unto the pond and bathed in the water. But a serpent smelled the fragrance of the plant. The serpent slithered forward silently and snatched the plant. As it snaked away, the serpent sloughed off its skin.

And then did Gilgamesh, when he beheld the serpent make away with the plant, sit himself upon the ground and weep. Down his cheeks did the tears flow. And Gilgamesh said unto Urshanabi, the Ferryman, "For what purpose, Urshanabi, have mine hands toiled? For what purpose has mine heart's blood been spent? No boon have I obtained for myself. Instead, a serpent has reaped the benefit thereof. And now do the floodtides rise for twenty leagues because I dug a shaft deep into the ground until the Abyss I did reach. How shall I now seek out the landmarks to return and find once again that plant? Let us abandon the boat upon the shore and continue on our journey."

After twenty leagues they broke bread. After thirty leagues they rested for the night. And then, at last, they came unto high wall'd Uruk. And Gilgamesh said to Urshanabi, the Ferryman, "Behold before you my city of Uruk. Observe well that mighty rampart which shines like unto copper. Behold the lower wall, which the works of none other may equal. Approach the threshold stone, ancient beyond remembrance. Draw near unto that Temple Eanna, dwelling-place of Goddess Ishtar. No King will ever surpass its like.

"Ascend the wall of Uruk and upon it walk. Examine the foundations, gaze upon the masonry. Were not the bricks fired in an oven and exceeding good? Did not the Seven Sages lay down its foundations?

"The length of one league is the city, one league is the date-grove, one league is the clay-pit, half a league is the Temple of Ishtar. Three leagues and a half is the measure of Uruk."

APPENDIX 1

Tablet XII

In those days, in those long ago days. In those nights, in those ancient nights. In those years, in those years of yesterday. In the old times, when what was needful had become known. In the old times, when what was needful had been fulfilled. When bread had been consumed in the sanctuaries of the realm. When the ovens of the realm had been fired up with bellows. When the Firmament had been split apart from the Earth. When the Earth had been split apart from the Firmament. When the name of Mankind had been settled. Then did Anu, Lord of the Gods, claim the Heavens for himself. And then did the Great God Enlil claim the Earth for himself. Whereupon did Anu bestow upon the Goddess Ereshkigal dominion over the Netherworld. And then did Ea, God of Wisdom, embark in his boat. Ea embarked in his boat on a journey unto the Netherworld. But then did a multitude of stones rain down upon Ea. Small stones rained down upon Ea. Large stones rained down upon Ea. The small stones were like unto hailstones. The large stones were like unto millstones. The stones rained down onto the deck of Ea's boat like a storm of pounding turtles. Against the God Ea, the waters before the boat howled as a wolf. Against the God Ea, the waters behind the boar roared as a lion.

And it came to pass, at that time, that there was a solitary tree, a lone poplar, which grew on the banks of the Holy Euphrates. From the river Euphrates did this tree draw water. But, during a tempest, the South Wind ripped out the roots of the tree and sundered its branches. And the waters of the Euphrates washed over this tree as it lay upon the ground. And it befell, one afternoon, as the Goddess Ishtar walked along the banks of the Euphrates, she did come to perceive this tree. The Goddess Ishtar venerated the word of Anu, Lord of the Gods. She venerated the word of the Great God Enlil. Whereupon did the Goddess Ishtar take the tree and carry it unto Uruk. She carried the tree unto the sacred garden of Ishtar. Therein did she plant the tree, not with her hand, but with her foot. Therein did she water the tree, not with her hand, but with her foot.

And then did the Goddess Ishtar exclaim, "How long ere there will be a splendid throne fashioned from the wood of this tree for me to sit upon?"

And then did the Goddess Ishtar exclaim, "How long ere there will be a splendid bed fashioned from the wood of this tree for me to lie upon?"

And then did five years come to pass. And then did ten years come to pass. And the poplar tree had grown immense, but the bark thereof had not split. But, in its base, a serpent that fears no curse had built its nest. In its branches, a giant Roc bird had hatched its young. In its trunk, a young Demon had made her dwelling-place.

And thus it befell that the Goddess Ishtar, the maiden who was wont to laugh with a joyous heart, wept instead.

As the first light of dawn appeared, the horizon grew bright. And the birds sang at the coming of day. And Shamash, the Sun God, did emerge from his bed-chamber. Whereupon did his sister, the Goddess Ishtar, speak thus unto Shamash, "O, my brother, in those days of long ago, when Destiny had been determined, when abundance overflowed the lands, when Anu, Lord of the Gods, had claimed the Heavens for himself, when the Great God Enlil had claimed the Earth for himself, when Anu did bestow upon the Goddess Ereshkigal dominion over the Netherworld, when Ea, God of Wisdom, embarked in his boat, when Ea embarked in his boat on a journey unto the Netherworld. Then did a multitude of stones rain down upon Ea. Small stones rained down upon Ea. Large stones rained down upon Ea. The small stones were like unto hailstones. The large stones were like unto millstones. The stones rained down onto the deck of Ea's boat like a storm of pounding turtles. Against the God Ea, the waters before the boat howled as a wolf. Against the God Ea, the waters behind the boar roared as a lion.

"And it came to pass, at that time, that there was a solitary tree, a lone poplar, which grew on the banks of the Holy Euphrates. From the river Euphrates did this tree draw water. But, during a tempest, the South Wind ripped out the roots of the tree and sundered its branches. And the waters of the Euphrates washed over this tree as it lay upon the ground. And it befell, one afternoon, as I walked along the banks of the Euphrates, I did come to perceive this tree. I venerate the word of Anu, Lord of the Gods. I venerate the word of the Great God Enlil. Whereupon did I take the tree and carry it unto Uruk. I carried the tree unto the sacred garden of Ishtar. Therein did I, the Goddess Ishtar, plant the tree, not with my hand, but with my foot. Therein did I, the Goddess Ishtar, water the tree, not with my hand, but with my foot.

"And then did I exclaim, 'How long ere there will be a splendid throne fashioned from the wood of this tree for me to sit upon?'

"And then did I exclaim, 'How long ere there will be a splendid bed fashioned from the wood of this tree for me to lie upon?'

"And then did five years come to pass. And then did ten years come to pass. And the poplar tree had grown immense, but its bark had not split. But, in its base, a serpent that fears no curse had built its nest. In its branches, a giant Roc bird had hatched its young. In its trunk, a young Demon had made her dwelling-place."

And thus it befell that the Goddess Ishtar, the maiden who was wont to laugh with a joyous heart, wept instead. But her brother, Shamash, the Sun God, deigned not to succor her in her affliction.

As the first light of dawn appeared, the horizon grew bright. And the birds sang at the coming of day. And Shamash, the Sun God, did emerge from his bed-chamber. Whereupon did his sister, the Goddess Ishtar, speak thus unto the warrior Gilgamesh, King of high-wall'd Uruk, "O, my brother, in those days of long ago, when Destiny had been determined, when abundance overflowed the lands, when Anu, Lord of the Gods, had claimed the Heavens for himself, when the Great God Enlil had claimed the Earth for himself, when Anu did bestow upon the Goddess Ereshkigal dominion over the Netherworld, when Ea, God of Wisdom, embarked in his boat, when Ea embarked in his boat on a journey unto the Netherworld. Then did a multitude of stones rain down upon Ea. Small stones rained down upon Ea. Large stones rained down upon Ea. The small stones were like unto hailstones. The large stones were like unto millstones. The stones rained down onto the deck of Ea's boat like a storm of pounding turtles. Against the God Ea, the waters before the boat howled as a wolf. Against the God Ea, the waters behind the boat roared as a lion.

"And it came to pass, at that time, that there was a solitary tree, a lone poplar, which grew on the banks of the Holy Euphrates. From the river Euphrates did this tree draw water. But, during a tempest, the South Wind ripped out the roots of the tree and sundered its branches. And the waters of the Euphrates washed over this tree as it lay upon the ground. And it befell, one afternoon, as I walked along the banks of the Euphrates, I did come to perceive this tree. I venerate the word of Anu, Lord of the Gods. I venerate the word of the Great God Enlil. Whereupon did I take the tree and carry it unto Uruk. I carried the tree unto the sacred garden of Ishtar. Therein did I, the Goddess Ishtar, plant the tree, not with my hand, but with my foot. Therein did I, the Goddess Ishtar, water the tree, not with my hand, but with my foot.

"And then did I exclaim, 'How long ere there will be a splendid throne fashioned from the wood of this tree for me to sit upon?'

"And then did I exclaim, 'How long ere there will be a splendid bed fashioned from the wood of this tree for me to lie upon?'

"And then did five years come to pass. And then did ten years come to pass. And the poplar tree had grown immense, but its bark had not split. But, in its base, a serpent that fears no curse had built its nest. In its branches, a giant Roc bird had hatched its young. In its trunk, a young Demon had made her dwelling-place."

And thus it befell that the Goddess Ishtar, the maiden who was wont to laugh with a joyous heart, wept instead. And it came to pass, when his sister spoke unto him in this manner, that her brother Gilgamesh deigned to succor her in her affliction.

About his loins, Gilgamesh girt himself with a garment which had a weight of fifty minas. To Gilgamesh, the weight of fifty minas was as light as thirty feathers. He took to hand his bronze axe which had a weight of seven talents and seven minas. And Gilgamesh smote, with his battle-axe, in the base of the poplar tree, the serpent that fears no curse. From the branches of the poplar tree, the giant Roc bird and its flock took flight and flew unto the highlands. In the trunk of the poplar tree, the young Demon abandoned her dwelling-place, and fled unto the wilderness. Whereupon, Gilgamesh tore out the tree from the ground by its roots, and also broke off its branches. And then the men of his city who had accompanied him chopped up the branches of the tree and bound them together.

And it came to pass that Gilgamesh bestowed upon his sister, the Goddess Ishtar, wood from the poplar tree for her throne. And also wood from the poplar tree for her bed.

And then did Gilgamesh carve, for himself, a ball from the base of the poplar tree, and a bat from the branch of the poplar tree. Gilgamesh toyed with the ball and took it unto the city square. He toyed with the bat and took it unto the city square. The youths of the city played a game with the ball. The youths of the city climbed upon the backs of orphans and played a game with the ball. The orphans groaned and cried out, "O my neck. O my back." The fortunate youth who had a mother, she brought him bread. The fortunate youth who had a sister, she poured him water.

As dusk grew near, Gilgamesh did mark the place where the ball had fallen. And then did he take up the ball and carry it unto his house. At dawn the day following, Gilgamesh placed the ball upon the mark he had made and took the bat to hand. But, at the plaints of the widows and the lamentations of the maidens, his ball and his bat fell down into the depths of the Netherworld. Gilgamesh tried with his hand, but he could not reach them. He tried with his foot, but he could not reach them. Gilgamesh seated himself before the Gate of Hell, the entrance to the Netherworld, and wept. Woeful tears did flow from his eyes.

And Gilgamesh cried, "O my ball. O my bat. O my ball, which I have not yet fully enjoyed. O my bat, which I have not yet fully enjoyed. Would that I had, this day, left my ball in the workshop of the woodworker. Would that I had, this day, left my ball with the woodworker's wife, who is like unto a mother to me. Would that I had, this day, left my ball with the woodworker's daughter, who is like unto a little sister to me. My ball has fallen down into the depths of the Netherworld. Who will bring up my ball from thence? My bat has fallen down into the depths of the Netherworld. Who will bring up my bat from thence?"

His friend Enkidu said unto Gilgamesh, "My Lord, why weep you so? Why be you heartsick? I myself shall, this day, fetch your ball from out of the Netherworld. I myself shall, this day, fetch your bat from out of the Netherworld."

Whereupon Gilgamesh said unto Enkidu, "If this day you descend into the Netherworld, I shall now proffer counsel to you. Heed well my advice. I will give you instructions. Give ear to my words. You must not don clean raiment. This will surely mark you as a visitor. Anoint not yourself with sweet unguents from the flagon, lest the inhabitants of the Netherworld encircle you when they scent it. Cast not your throw-stick in the Netherworld, lest those hit by the throw-stick encircle you. Carry not a staff in your hand, lest the ghosts of the Netherworld hover about you. Put not shoes under your foot sole, lest in the Netherworld it does make a loud echo. Your wife, whom you love, kiss her not. Your wife, whom you hate, chastise her not. Your son, whom you love, kiss him not. Your son, whom you hate, chastise him not, for the Dirge of the Dead will surely overcome you, 'She who lies there. She who lies there. The Mother of Ninazu, God of Death, who sleeps there, she wears no garment upon her luminous shoulders. Upon her splendid bosom is no linen spread. Her fingernails she wields like a weapon. Her hair has the appearance of leeks.' "

But Enkidu heeded not these words of Gilgamesh. Ere his journey unto the Netherworld, Enkidu donned clean raiment. This did mark him as a visitor to the Netherworld. He anointed himself with sweet unguents from the flagon, and the inhabitants of the Netherworld encircled him when they scented it. He did cast his throw-stick in the Netherworld, and those hit by the throw-stick did encircle him. He did carry a staff in his hand, and the ghosts of the Netherworld hovered about him. He put shoes under his foot sole, and it did make a loud echo in the Netherworld. His wife, whom he loved, he did kiss. His wife, whom he hated, he did chastise. His son, whom he loved, he did kiss. His son, whom he hated, he did chastise. And, forsooth, the Dirge of the Dead did overcome him, 'She who lies there. She who lies there. The Mother of Ninazu, God of Death, who sleeps there, she wears no garment upon her luminous shoulders. Upon her splendid bosom is no linen spread. Her fingernails she wields like a weapon. Her hair has the appearance of leeks.'

From that ill-fated day unto the seventh day thereafter, Enkidu ascended not from the Netherworld. And Gilgamesh did utter a sorrowful wail and sob bitter tears. And Gilgamesh cried out, "My beloved friend, my devoted comrade, the one who counselled me, the Netherworld has seized him. Namtar, God of Fate, did not seize him. Asag, God of Fever, did not seize him. The Netherworld seized him. Nergal, God of Pestilence, did not seize him. The Netherworld seized him. Neither did he fall in combat upon the field of battle, as a valorous warrior should. The Netherworld seized him."

And then did Gilgamesh, son of the Goddess Ninsun, wend his way alone unto Ekur, Temple of the Great God Enlil. And there did Gilgamesh weep and cry out unto the Great God Enlil, "O my father Enlil, my ball has fallen into the Netherworld. My bat has fallen into the Netherworld. Enkidu journeyed unto the Netherworld to retrieve them, but the Netherworld seized him. My beloved friend, my devoted comrade, the one who counselled me, the Netherworld has seized him. Namtar, God of Fate, did not seize him. Asag, God of Fever, did not seize him. The Netherworld seized him. Nergal, God of Pestilence, did not seize him. The Netherworld seized him. Neither did he fall in combat upon the field of battle, as a valorous warrior should. The Netherworld seized him."

But the Great God Enlil deigned not to succor Gilgamesh in his anguish. So Gilgamesh betook himself alone unto the city of Ur, dwelling-place of Sin, God of the Moon. And there did Gilgamesh weep and cry out unto Sin, God of the Moon, "O my father Sin, my ball has fallen into the Netherworld. My bat has fallen into the Netherworld. Enkidu journeyed unto the Netherworld to retrieve them, but the Netherworld seized him. My beloved friend, my devoted comrade, the one who counselled me, the Netherworld has seized him. Namtar, God of Fate, did not seize him. Asag, God of Fever, did not seize him. The Netherworld seized him. Nergal, God of Pestilence, did not seize him. The Netherworld seized him. Neither did he fall in combat upon the field of battle, as a valorous warrior should. The Netherworld seized him."

But Sin, God of the Moon, deigned not to succor Gilgamesh in his anguish. So Gilgamesh betook himself alone unto the Temple of Eridu, dwelling-place of Ea, God of Wisdom. And there did Gilgamesh weep and cry out unto Ea, God of Wisdom, "O my father Ea, my ball has fallen into the Netherworld. My bat has fallen into the Netherworld. Enkidu journeyed unto the Netherworld to retrieve them, but the Netherworld seized him. My beloved friend, my devoted comrade, the one who counselled me, the Netherworld has seized him. Namtar, God of Fate, did not seize him. Asag, God of Fever, did not seize him. The Netherworld seized him. Nergal, God of Pestilence, did not seize him. The Netherworld seized him. Neither did he fall in combat upon the field of battle, as a valorous warrior should. The Netherworld seized him."

And it befell that Ea, God of Wisdom, did deign to succor Gilgamesh in his anguish. Whereupon Ea spoke thus unto the young warrior Utu, son of the Goddess Ningal, "Open now a hole into the Netherworld, that the spirit of Enkidu may ascend and issue forth from the Netherworld in order to have speech with Gilgamesh."

The young warrior Utu, son of the Goddess Ningal, gave ear to the words of Ea. And then did Utu open a hole into the Netherworld, and the spirit of Enkidu ascended and issued forth from the Netherworld. Whereupon did Gilgamesh and Enkidu behold each other, and wail and moan.

Gilgamesh said, "Tell me, O my friend, tell me, O my friend, tell me what you have witnessed of the ways of the Netherworld."

Enkidu said, "Nay, my friend, I will not tell you. Nay, my friend, I will not tell you. Were I to tell you what I have witnessed of the ways of the Netherworld, you would surely sit yourself down and weep."

Gilgamesh said, "Then I shall sit myself down and I shall weep."

Enkidu said, "My body, which once you were pleased to embrace, has now moldered into putrefaction. My body, which once you were pleased to embrace, has now become unto dust. Like an aged garment, my body is infested with maggots. Like a crack in the floor, my body is filled with dirt."

Gilgamesh said, "O woeful Fate." Gilgamesh seated himself upon the ground and wept, and he said unto Enkidu, "Saw you the man with one son?"

Enkidu said, "I saw him."

Gilgamesh said, "How fares he?"

Enkidu said, "He weeps in sorrow, for his house has been sold."

Gilgamesh said, "Saw you the man with two sons?"

Enkidu said, "I saw him."

Gilgamesh said, "How fares he?"

Enkidu said, "He sits upon two bricks and eats a loaf of bread."

Gilgamesh said, "Saw you the man with three sons?"

Enkidu said, "I saw him."

Gilgamesh said, "How fares he?"

Enkidu said, "He quaffs plentiful swallows of water from a water-skin hung upon his saddle."

Gilgamesh said, "Saw you the man with four sons?"

Enkidu said, "I saw him."

Gilgamesh said, "How fares he?"

Enkidu said, "His heart does rejoice like a man with a wagon drawn by four asses."

Gilgamesh said, "Saw you the man with five sons?"

Enkidu said, "I saw him."

Gilgamesh said, "How fares he?"

Enkidu said, "His hand is like unto that of an accomplished scribe. He enters into the Palace unmolested."

Gilgamesh said, "Saw you the man with six sons?"

Enkidu said, "I saw him."

Gilgamesh said, "How fares he?"

Enkidu said, "His heart exults, like unto the man who guides his fruitful plow along the furrow."

Gilgamesh said, "Saw you the man with seven sons?"

Enkidu said, "I saw him."

Gilgamesh said, "How fares he?"

Enkidu said, "Upon a throne in the midst of the lesser Deities does he sit, and he hears the petitions of claimants who bring grievances before him."

Gilgamesh said, "Saw you the man with no son?"

Enkidu said, "I saw him."

Gilgamesh said, "How fares he?"

Enkidu said, "He fares poorly, for he has no son to mourn him. Bitter bread does he eat, hard as a kiln-fired brick."

Gilgamesh said, "Saw you the Royal Courtier?"

Enkidu said, "I saw him."

Gilgamesh said, "How fares he?"

Enkidu said, "Like unto a useless staff, he leans against a corner."

Gilgamesh said, "Saw you the woman who has never given birth to a child?"

Enkidu said, "I saw her."

Gilgamesh said, "How fares she?"

Enkidu said, "Like unto a defective vessel, she is cast aside. No man does take pleasure in her."

Gilgamesh said, "Saw you the young man who uncovered not the loins of his wife?"

Enkidu said, "I saw him."

Gilgamesh said, "How fares he?"

Enkidu said, "For all eternity does he knot ropes and then does he undo these knots. And, for all eternity, does he cry over this."

Gilgamesh said, "Saw you the young woman who uncovered not the loins of her husband?"

Enkidu said, "I saw her."

Gilgamesh said, "How fares she?"

Enkidu said, "For all eternity does she braid reeds and then does she undo these braids. And, for all eternity, does she cry over this."

Gilgamesh said, "Saw you the leper?"

Enkidu said, "I saw him."

Gilgamesh said, "How fares he?"

Enkidu said, "His food is set apart from the others. His drink is set apart from the others. He eats chaff and offal from the ground. He laps up fetid water from the ground. He dwells apart from the city."

Gilgamesh said, "Saw you the man afflicted with the palsy?"

Enkidu said, "I saw him."

Gilgamesh said, "How fares he?"

Enkidu said, "Like unto an ox does he twitch as the vermin eat him."

Gilgamesh said, "Saw you the man who was devoured by a lion?"

Enkidu said, "I saw him."

Gilgamesh said, "How fares he?"

Enkidu said, "In sorrow does he cry out, 'O my hand. O my foot.' "

Gilgamesh said, "Saw you the man who has fallen from a roof?"

Enkidu said, "I saw him."

Gilgamesh said, "How fares he?"

Enkidu said, "His broken bones cannot be healed."

Gilgamesh said, "Saw you the man whom the Storm God drowned?"

Enkidu said, "I saw him."

Gilgamesh said, "How fares he?"

Enkidu said, "Like unto an ox does he twitch as the vermin eat him."

Gilgamesh said, "Saw you the man who honored not the words of his mother and his father?"

Enkidu said, "I saw him."

Gilgamesh said, "How fares he?"

Enkidu said, "He drinks water measured out by the spoonful, but never is his thirst slaked."

Gilgamesh said, "Saw you the man who was accursed by his mother and his father?"

Enkidu said, "I saw him."

Gilgamesh said, "How fares he?"

Enkidu said, "No heir has he, and so his spirit shall forever wander."

Gilgamesh said, "Saw you the man who has fallen in battle?"

Enkidu said, "I saw him."

Gilgamesh said, "How fares he?"

Enkidu said, "His father and his mother do cradle his head, while his wife does weep and wail."

Gilgamesh said, "Saw you the man whose corpse was left to decompose in the desert?"

Enkidu said, "I saw him not. His spirit reposes not in the Netherworld."

Gilgamesh said, "Saw you the ghost of the man who has no one alive to make funerary offerings for him?"

Enkidu said, "I saw him."

Gilgamesh said, "How fares he?"

Enkidu said, "Scraps from the table and broken bread from the gutter does he eat."

Gilgamesh said, "Saw you the tiny stillborn babies, who never knew their own names?"

Enkidu said, "I saw them."

Gilgamesh said, "How fare they?"

Enkidu said, "Upon tables of silver and gold do they frolic, and butter and honey do they eat."

Gilgamesh said, "Saw you the youth struck down in his prime?"

Enkidu said, "I saw him."

Gilgamesh said, "How fares he?"

Enkidu said, "Upon the bed of the Gods does he lie."

Gilgamesh said, "Saw you the man who was consumed by the flames?"

Enkidu said, "I saw him not. His spirit was not in the Netherworld. It ascended unto the Heavens in smoke."

Gilgamesh said, "Saw you the man who deceived a God and swore a false oath?"

Enkidu said, "I saw him."

Gilgamesh said, "How fares he?"

Enkidu said, "He is unable to partake of libation offerings in the Netherworld. From eternal thirst does he suffer."

Gilgamesh said, "Saw you the man of Girsu at the place of mourning for his father and his mother?"

Enkidu said, "I saw him."

Gilgamesh said, "How fares he?"

Enkidu said, "A thousand Amorites confront him. His ghost cannot smite them. He cannot vanquish them. At the places of libation offerings in the Netherworld, the Amorites stand before him and block his entry."

Gilgamesh said, "Saw you the Sumerians and the Akkadians?"

Enkidu said, "I saw them."

Gilgamesh said, "How fare they?"

Enkidu said, "Amidst the carnage upon the field of battle, malodorous water do they drink."

Gilgamesh said, "Saw you my mother and my father in the place wherein they dwell?"

Enkidu said, "I saw them."

Gilgamesh said, "How fare they?"

Enkidu said, "Amidst the carnage upon the field of battle, the two of them do drink of malodorous water."

Therefore did Gilgamesh return unto high-wall'd Uruk. He journeyed unto his city. And then did Gilgamesh command that war-gear and armor and weapons be placed into storage. And then a great festival did Gilgamesh decree to be

celebrated in his palace. The young men and the young women of Uruk, and the
Elders and the matrons, beheld the statues of the mother and the father of
Gilgamesh, and their hearts did rejoice.

And it came to pass that Gilgamesh turned his face toward Shamash, the Sun
God, who issued forth from his bed-chamber in the morn.

Gilgamesh uttered this incantation, "O my father, O my mother, drink you of
this clear water."

Not half done was the day when Gilgamesh removed his crown. Then did
Gilgamesh prostrate himself and proceed to perform the mourning rituals. For the
space of seven days did Gilgamesh prostrate himself and perform the mourning
rituals. And, for the space of seven days, did the young men and the young women
of Uruk, and the Elders and the matrons, weep sorrowful tears. And it befell as
Gilgamesh had said, for the multitudes wailed this incantation, as Gilgamesh had
done, "O my father, O my mother, drink you of this clear water."

And the multitudes chanted, "O intrepid warrior Gilgamesh, son of the
Goddess Ninsun, how sweet it is to sing your praises."

APPENDIX 2

THE DEATH OF GILGAMESH

The Great Wild Bull has lain himself down. He shall never arise again. The Lord Gilgamesh has lain himself down. He shall never arise again. He who was unvanquished in battle shall never arise again. Gilgamesh, the undaunted warrior, strong of arm, shall never arise again. He who was unequaled in might has lain himself down. He shall never arise again. He who smote the wicked has lain himself down. He shall never arise again. He who had wisdom beyond measure has lain himself down. He shall never arise again. Gilgamesh, who climbed the highest mountain, has lain himself down. He shall never arise again. The Lord of Kullab, dwelling-place of the Wild Cow Goddess Ninsun, has lain himself down. He shall never arise again. Gilgamesh has lain himself down upon his death-bed. He shall never arise again. He has lain himself down upon a bed of sorrow. He shall never arise again.

Gilgamesh is unable to stand. He is unable to sit. He can only lament. Gilgamesh is unable to eat. He is unable to drink. He can only lament. Namtar, God of Death and Disease, has caught Gilgamesh in his clutches. Gilgamesh is unable to arise. Like unto a fish trapped in a net, Gilgamesh is unable to escape. Like unto a gazelle trapped in a snare, Gilgamesh is unable to escape. Namtar, God of Death and Disease, who has no hand, who has no foot, is wont to seize a man in the night. Namtar has taken hold of Gilgamesh.

For the space of six days did Gilgamesh lie upon his sick-bed. Great drops of sweat rolled down his face and his body. As Lord Gilgamesh lay ill, a heartfelt cry of lamentation was raised in the cities of Uruk and Kullab. Word of his illness spread swiftly throughout the Kingdom. As the young Lord Gilgamesh lay upon his death-bed, a dream came unto him.

In that dream, Ea, God of Wisdom, did summon Gilgamesh to appear before the ceremonial assembly-place of the Gods. As Lord Gilgamesh drew near unto that holy site of the Gods, they said to him, "O Gilgamesh, you have travelled afar. Along all roads have you journeyed. The mighty Cedar Tree did you carry down from the mountain. You slew Humbaba, the Fierce, in the Forest of Cedars. You did erect monuments for men to gaze upon in ages to come. You did consecrate the Temples of the Gods. You journeyed afar and reached Utanapishtim, the Immortal One, who survived the Great Flood. It was you who did restore, unto the people, the archaic and forgotten rites of ancient Sumer. You did ordain the prescribed sacraments of purification. You brought back knowledge of what obtained before the Great Flood, and made known what was needful for the land."

And Gilgamesh stood before the Gods. And the Gods related unto Ea, God of Wisdom, the wishes of the Great God Enlil. Whereupon did Ea make reply unto Enlil and Anu, Lord of the Gods, in this manner, "In those days, in those long ago days. In those nights, in those ancient nights. In those years, in those years of yesterday. In the old times, after the Assembly of Gods had caused the Great Deluge to sweep over the land and destroy the race of men, yet did one man survive. Utanapishtim, the Immortal One, one of mankind, did still live. From that day until this, we affirmed, by the life of Heaven and the life of Earth, from that day until this, we affirmed that no man should have life eternal. Now is Gilgamesh brought to stand before us. Notwithstanding that his mother be the Wild Cow Goddess Ninsun, we cannot grant him eternal life. However, Gilgamesh, as a ghost in the Netherworld, shall assume the role of Governor of that realm. He shall rule over the ghosts in the Netherworld. Gilgamesh will render judgment, he will issue verdicts. His word shall be as weighty as that of the Gods Ningishzida and Dumuzi."

Then was distressed the heart of the young Lord, the Lord Gilgamesh, when he knew that his life-days had come to an end. The God of Dreams, Sissig, son of the Sun God, Shamash, would be as his light in the Netherworld, that place of darkness. And those men, who are recalled by name, when their memorial statues are erected in times to come, then shall those selfsame youths and warriors undergo tests of strength and skill. During the Month of Torches, the Ceremony of Ghosts, since Sissig is not present, no light shall there be.

In that dream, the Great God Enlil, Father of the Gods, spoke unto Lord Gilgamesh in this manner, "O Gilgamesh, your Destiny was to be a King. But life everlasting was not ordained for you. Be not heart-sick that your allotted life-days must come to an end. Let not your spirit be aggrieved. Let not your breast be distressed. The Fate of all men has, at last, come to you, as I have decreed. At the moment your birth-cord was cut, as I have decreed, this was to be your Destiny. Now has the unhappiest day of all men overtaken you. Now has the loneliest day of all men overtaken you. Now has the inevitable flood-tide that overwhelms all men overtaken you. Now has the battle from which there is no escape overtaken you. Now has the foe who cannot be vanquished overtaken you. Now has the struggle from which there is no exculpation overtaken you.

"But descend not unto that Great City with wrath entwining your heart. Let Shamash, the Sun God, untwine and disentangle wrath from your heart. Let him undo wrath from your heart like the strands of the palm tree. Like unto the layers of an onion, let him peel wrath away. Hie yourself unto the funerary feast where sit the assembly of the Great Anunna Gods. Go you unto the domain wherein the High Priests sit. Go you unto the domain wherein the lesser priests sit. Go you unto the domain wherein the Lumah-Priests, who are chosen by means of omens, sit. Go you unto the domain wherein the Lady Divine Priestesses, who receive foodstuffs, sit. Go you unto the domain wherein the linen-clothed Guda-Priest is anointed. Go you unto the domain wherein the True One abides. That is the place wherein you may find your father. That is the place wherein you may find your grandfather. That is the place wherein you may find your mother and your sister. That is the place wherein you shall encounter your beloved companion, Enkidu, your constant friend and stalwart comrade in arms.

"There, in that Great City, dwell Kings and Emperors unnumbered. There likewise dwell Generals of Armies and Commanders of Cavalries. From your sister's house will your sister issue forth to greet you. From your brother's house will your brother issue forth to greet you. From your beloved companion's house will Enkidu issue forth to greet you. Your dear friend, Enkidu, will come forth to greet you. The Elders of your city of Uruk will come forth to greet you.

"Let not your spirit despair. Be not heart-sick with desolation. For now shall you be counted as one of the Anunna Gods. You will be numbered as one of the lesser Deities. As Governor of the Netherworld shall you be styled. You will render judgment, you will issue verdicts. Your word shall be as weighty as that of the Gods Ningishzida and Dumuzi."

Then did the young Lord, Lord Gilgamesh, awaken from his dream. And then did Gilgamesh shudder. It had been a deep sleep. His eyes did he rub. All about him was a mournful silence. The dream was inauspicious. Whereupon did Gilgamesh, Lord of Kullab, Hero of the Shining Mountain, King of Uruk, Handiwork of the Great Gods, seek the advice of his counselors, unto whom he related his dream in this manner, "By the life of the mother who gave birth to me, the Great Wild Cow Goddess Ninsun, and the father who begot me, the virtuous King Lugalbanda, and my Ea, God of Wisdom, shall I suck like a mewling baby at the breast of the mother who bore me? My Fate has been decreed by the Great God Enlil. Namtar, God of Death and Disease, who has no hand, who has no foot, who is wont to seize a man in the night, has taken hold of me.

"In my dream, Ea, God of Wisdom, did summon me to appear before the holy assembly-place of the Gods. And there, as I drew near, did the Gods say unto me, 'O Gilgamesh, you have travelled afar. Along all roads have you journeyed. The mighty Cedar Tree did you carry down from the mountain. You slew Humbaba, the Fierce, in the Forest of Cedars. You did erect monuments for men to gaze upon in ages to come. You did consecrate the Temples of the Gods. You journeyed afar and reached Utanapishtim, the Immortal One, who survived the Great Flood. It was you who did restore, unto the people, the archaic and forgotten rites of ancient Sumer. You did ordain the prescribed sacraments of purification. You brought back knowledge of what obtained before the Great Flood, and made known what was needful for the land.'

"And I stood before the Gods. And the Gods related unto Ea, God of Wisdom, the wishes of the Great God Enlil. Whereupon did Ea make reply unto Enlil and Anu, Lord of the Gods, in this manner, 'In those days, in those long ago days. In those nights, in those ancient nights. In those years, in those years of yesterday. In the old times, after the Assembly of Gods had caused the Great Deluge to sweep over the land and destroy the race of men, yet did one man survive. Utanapishtim, the Immortal One, one of mankind, did still live. From that day until this, we affirmed, by the life of Heaven and the life of Earth, from that day until this, we affirmed that no man should have life eternal. Now is Gilgamesh brought to stand before us. Notwithstanding that his mother be the Wild Cow Goddess Ninsun, we cannot grant him eternal life. However, Gilgamesh, as a ghost in the Netherworld, shall assume the role of Governor of that realm. He shall rule over the ghosts in the Netherworld. Gilgamesh will render judgment, he will issue verdicts. His word shall be as weighty as that of the Gods Ningishzida and Dumuzi.'

"Then was distressed my heart when I knew that my life-days had come to an end. The God of Dreams, Sissig, son of the Sun God, Shamash, would be as my light in the Netherworld, that place of darkness. And those men, who are recalled by name, when their memorial statues are erected in times to come, then shall those selfsame youths and warriors undergo tests of strength and skill. During the Month of Torches, the Ceremony of Ghosts, since Sissig is not present, no light shall there be.

"In my dream, the Great God Enlil, Father of the Gods, spoke unto me in this manner, 'O Gilgamesh, your Destiny was to be a King. But life everlasting was not ordained for you. Be not heart-sick that your allotted life-days must come to an end. Let not your spirit be aggrieved. Let not your breast be distressed. The Fate of all men has, at last, come to you, as I have decreed. At the moment your birth-cord was cut, as I have decreed, this was to be your Destiny. Now has the unhappiest day of all men overtaken you. Now has the loneliest day of all men overtaken you. Now has the inevitable flood-tide that overwhelms all men overtaken you. Now has the battle from which there is no escape overtaken you. Now has the foe who cannot be vanquished overtaken you. Now has the struggle from which there is no exculpation overtaken you.

'But descend not unto that Great City with wrath entwining your heart. Let Shamash, the Sun God, untwine and disentangle wrath from your heart. Let him undo wrath from your heart like the strands of the palm tree. Like unto the layers of an onion, let him peel wrath away. Hie yourself unto the funerary feast where sit the assembly of the Great Anunna Gods. Go you unto the domain wherein the High Priests sit. Go you unto the domain wherein the lesser priests sit. Go you unto the domain wherein the Lumah-Priests, who are chosen by means of omens, sit. Go you unto the domain wherein the Lady Divine Priestesses, who receive foodstuffs, sit. Go you unto the domain wherein the linen-clothed Guda-Priest is anointed. Go you unto the domain wherein the True One abides. That is the place wherein you may find your father. That is the place wherein you may find your grandfather. That is the place wherein you may find your mother and your sister. That is the place wherein you shall encounter your beloved companion, Enkidu, your constant friend and stalwart comrade in arms.

'There, in that Great City, dwell Kings and Emperors unnumbered. There likewise dwell Generals of Armies and Commanders of Cavalries. From your sister's house will your sister issue forth to greet you. From your brother's house will your brother issue forth to greet you. From your beloved companion's house will Enkidu issue forth to greet you. Your dear friend, Enkidu, will come forth to greet you. The Elders of your city of Uruk will come forth to greet you.

'Let not your spirit despair. Be not heart-sick with desolation. For now shall you be counted as one of the Anunna Gods. You will be numbered as one of the lesser Deities. As Governor of the Netherworld shall you be styled. You will render judgment, you will issue verdicts. Your word shall be as weighty as that of the Gods Ningishzida and Dumuzi.' "

After the young Lord, the Lord Gilgamesh, the Lord of Kullab, had recounted his dream unto his counselors, they did make reply unto Gilgamesh thus, "O, Lord Gilgamesh, why weep you so? For what reason do you cry? Never has the Birth Goddess borne a man whom Death has not yet seized. Never, since the first man walked upon the Earth, has there ever been such a one. Even unto the greatest warrior must Death appear. A bird of the sky, once caught in the trap, cannot fly away. A fish of the sea, once caught in the net, cannot swim away. No man, whomsoever he may be, can ascend from the depths of the Netherworld. Even from days of yore, who has ever witnessed such a thing? There has never been, and shall never be, another King who has been decreed a Destiny such as yours. Of all men, of those who are recalled by name, who can be compared to you? You shall be styled Governor of the Netherworld. You shall be counted as one of the Anunna Gods. You will render judgment, you will issue verdicts. Your word shall be as weighty as that of the Gods Ningishzida and Dumuzi."

And it befell that Gilgamesh had a dream concerning the construction of his tomb. And Gilgamesh commanded that his tomb be built as he had dreamed. Lord Gilgamesh issued a decree in his city. Whereupon did the Herald sound his outcry in all the land, thus, "O Uruk, arise. Breach the dikes of the Euphrates. O Kullab, arise. Let flow out the waters of the Euphrates."

And the waters of Uruk flowed in a mighty deluge. And the waters of Kullab were as a great miasma. Not a fortnight did pass. Not ten days did pass. Not five days did pass. When the Euphrates was breached, its waters rushed forth. The shells in the river bed beheld the Sun God in wonderment. Cracked and dry lay the floor of the River Euphrates.

In the bed of the River Euphrates did Gilgamesh erect his sepulcher of stone. He built its walls of stone. He made its doors of stone. The bolt and threshold thereof were made of granite. The beams thereof were cast in gold. The floor thereof was constructed of great blocks of stone. This burial chamber would be cleverly concealed so that, in ages to come, no man would ever encounter it. No man who searched for the Tomb of Gilgamesh would ever be able to discover its sacred location. Thus did the young Lord, Lord Gilgamesh, establish, within the confines of Uruk, a safeguarded crypt for all time.

And then did Lord Gilgamesh bury with him, in his tomb, his beloved wife, his beloved son, his beloved second wife, his beloved concubine, his beloved minstrel, his beloved steward, his beloved barber, his beloved courtiers, his beloved servants and his beloved possessions. All were interred at their proper stations, as if within the palace of Gilgamesh in Uruk. All would accompany him on his journey unto the Netherworld.

And then did Gilgamesh, son of the Wild Cow Goddess Ninsun, set out offerings for the Goddess Ereshkigal, Queen of the Netherworld, and for all the Gods of the Dead. He set out offerings for Namtar, God of Death and Disease. He set out offerings for the God Dimpikug, Chair-Bearer of the Netherworld. He set out offerings for the God Bitti, Gate-Keeper of the Netherworld. He set out offerings for the Gods Ningishzida and Dumuzi, for Ea, God of Wisdom, and for Ninki, for Enmul and Ninmul, for Endukugga and Nindukugga, for Endashurima and Nindashurima, for Enutila and Enmeshara, all the ancestral Gods, all the forebears of the Great God Enlil. He set out an offering for Shulpae, God of Feasts. He set out an offering for Sumuqan, God of Animals. He set out an offering for Aruru, Goddess of Birth. He set out an offering for the Anunna Gods of the Sacred Mount. He set out an offering for the Lower Gods of the Sacred Mount. He set out an offering for the dead High Priests. He set out an offering for the dead lesser priests. He set out an offering for the dead Lumah-Priests. He set out an offering for the dead Lady Divine Priestesses. He set out an offering for the dead Guda-Priest.

And then did Gilgamesh lay himself down upon his death-bed, inlaid with gold. Lord Gilgamesh, son of the Great Wild Cow Goddess Ninsun, then poured a libation of wine unto the Gods, and departed from this life to begin his journey hence. Whereupon, the people of Uruk did carry the body of their dead Lord unto his tomb. The door thereof they did seal. The dikes of the River Euphrates did they breach. The waters of the great river washed over the sepulcher and covered the tomb from view. Thus, hidden for all Eternity, was the burial chamber of Gilgamesh.

And the multitudes, for the Young Lord, for the Lord Gilgamesh, did gnash their teeth in sorrow. The multitudes did tear out their hair in anguish. The multitudes did rend their garments and smear their faces with dirt. For the Young Lord, for the Lord Gilgamesh, the multitudes despaired. Their hearts were afflicted. Their spirits were distressed.

Those men, who are recalled by name, whose memorial statues have been erected since days of yore and placed in shrines in the Temples of the Gods, may their names be remembered for all Eternity and never forgotten. The Great Goddess Aruru, Mother of All Birth, sister of the Great God Enlil, gave men sons to carry on their names. Their memorial statues, carved since olden times, shall proclaim their renown throughout all the land.

O Goddess Ereshkigal, Queen of the Netherworld, mother of the God Ninazu, how sweet it is to sing your praises.

AFTERWORD

THE EPIC OF GILGAMESH
BY
R. CAMPBELL THOMPSON, M.A., D. Litt., F.S.A.

The Epic of Gilgamesh, written in cuneiform on Assyrian and Babylonian clay tablets, is one of the most interesting poems in the world. It is of great antiquity, and, inasmuch as a fragment of a Sumerian Deluge text is extant, it would appear to have had its origin with the Sumerians at a remote period, perhaps the fourth millennium, or even earlier. Three tablets of it exist written in Semitic (Akkadian), which cannot be much later than 2000 B.C. Half a millennium later come the remains of editions from Boghaz Keui, the Hittite capital in the heart of Asia Minor, written not only in Akkadian, but also in Hittite and another dialect. After these comes the tablet found at Ashur, the old Assyrian capital, which is anterior in date to the great editions now preserved in the British Museum, which were made in the seventh century B.C. for the Royal Library at Nineveh, one Sinliqiunninni being one of the editors. Finally, there are small neo-Babylonian fragments representing still later editions.

In the seventh century edition, which forms the main base of our knowledge of the poem, it was divided into twelve tablets, each containing about three hundred lines in metre. Its subject was the Legend of Gilgamesh, a composite story made up probably of different myths which had grown up at various times around the hero's name. He was one of the earliest Kings of Erech in the South of Babylonia, and his name is found written on a tablet giving the rulers of Erech, following in order after that of Tammuz (the god of vegetation and one of the husbands of Ishtar), who, in his turn, follows Lugalbanda, the tutelary god of the House of Gilgamesh. The mother of Gilgamesh was Ninsun. According to the Epic, long ago in the old days of Babylonia (perhaps 5000 B.C.), when all the cities had their own kings, and each state rose and fell according to the ability of its ruler, Gilgamesh is holding Erech in thrall, and the inhabitants appeal to the Gods to be relieved from his tyranny. To aid them, the wild man Enkidu is created, and he, seduced by the wiles of one of the dancing girls of the Temple of Ishtar, is enticed into the great city, where at once (it would appear) by ancient right Gilgamesh attempts to rob him of his love. A tremendous fight ensues, and mutual admiration of each other's prowess follows, to so great an extent that the two heroes become firm friends and determine to make an expedition together to the Forest of Cedars, which is guarded by an ogre, Humbaba, to carry off the cedar wood for the adornment of the city. They encounter Humbaba and, by the help of the Sun-God who sends the winds to their aid, capture him and cut off his head. And then, with this exploit, the goddess Ishtar, letting her eye rest on the handsome Gilgamesh, falls in love with him. But he rebuffs her proposal to wed him with contumely and she, indignant at the insult, begs her father Anu to make a divine bull to destroy the two heroes. This bull, capable of killing three hundred men at one blast of his fiery breath, is overcome by Enkidu, who thus incurs the punishment of hubris at the hands of the gods, who decide that, although Gilgamesh may be spared, Enkidu must die.

With the death of his friend, Gilgamesh, in horror at the thought of similar extinction, goes in search of eternal life and, after much adventuring, meets first with Siduri, a goddess who makes wine, whose philosophy of life, as she gives it to him, however sensible, is evidently intended to smack of the hedonism of the Bacchante. Then he meets with Urshanabi (the boatman of Utanapishtim) who may perhaps have been introduced as a second philosopher to give his advice to the hero. Conceivably he has been brought into the story because of the sails (?) [Beings of Stone] which would have carried them over the Waters of Death (by means of the winds, the Breath of Life?), if Gilgamesh had not previously destroyed them with this own hand.

Finally comes the meeting with Utanapishtim (Noah) who tells Gilgamesh the story of the Flood, and how the gods gave him, the one man saved, the gift of eternal life. But who can do this for Gilgamesh, who is so human as to be overcome by sleep? No, all Utanapishtim can do is to tell him of a plant at the bottom of the sea which will make him young again, and, to obtain this plant, Gilgamesh, tying stones to his feet in the manner of Bahrain pearl-divers, dives into the water. Successful, he sets off home with his plant, but, while he is washing at a chance pool, a snake snatches it from him, and he is again frustrated in his quest, and nothing now is left him, save to seek a way of summoning Enkidu back from Hades, which he tries to do by transgressing every taboo known to those who mourn for the dead. Ultimately, at the bidding of the God of the Underworld, Enkidu comes forth and pictures the sad fate of the dead in the Underworld to his friend and, on this sombre note, the tragedy ends.

Of the poetic beauty of the Epic there is no need to speak. Expressed in a language which has perhaps the simplicity, not devoid of cumbrousness, of Hebrew, rather than the flexibility of Greek, it can nevertheless describe the whole range of human emotions in the aptest language, from the love of a mother for her son, to the fear of death in the primitive mind of one who has just seen his friend die, to the anger of a woman scorned.

To George Smith, one of the greatest geniuses Assyriology has produced, science owes much for the first arrangement and translations of the text of this extraordinary poem. Indeed, it was for this Epic that he sacrificed his life, for actually it was the discovery of the Deluge Tablet in the British Museum Collections which led the Daily Telegraph to subscribe so generously for the re-opening of the diggings in the hope of further finds at Kouyunjik (Nineveh), in conducting which he died all too early in 1876. Sir Henry Rawlinson and Professor Pinches played no small part in the reconstruction and publication of at least two of the tablets, and, to their labors in this field, must be added the ingenuity of Professor Sayce and the solid acumen of Dr. L. W. King. In America, to Professor Haupt is owed the first complete edition of the texts, very accurately copied, and later on the editions of two early Babylonian texts were edited by Langdon, Clay and Jastrow. Among German publications must be mentioned the translations of Jensen and Ungnad, with the edition of an old Babylonian tablet by Meissner. The Boghaz Keui texts have been edited by Weidner, Friedrich and Ungnad.

In the year 1914, the University Museum secured by purchase a large six column tablet nearly complete, carrying originally, according to the scribal note, 240 lines of text. The contents supply the South Babylonian version of the second book of the epic *Sa Nagba Imuru,* "He who has seen all things," commonly referred to as the Epic of Gilgamesh. The tablet is said to have been found at Senkere, ancient Larsa near Warka, modern Arabic name for and vulgar descendant of the ancient name Uruk, the Biblical Erech mentioned in Genesis X. This fact makes the new text the more interesting since the legend of Gilgamesh is said to have originated at Erech and the hero in fact figures as one of the prehistoric Sumerian rulers of that ancient city. The dynastic list preserved on a Nippur tablet mentions him as the fifth king of a legendary line of rulers at Erech who succeeded the dynasty of Kish, a city in North Babylonia near the more famous but more recent city Babylon. The list at Erech contains the names of two well-known Sumerian deities, Lugalbanda and Tammuz. The reign of the former is given at 1,200 years, and that of Tammuz at 100 years. Gilgamesh ruled 126 years. We have to do here with a confusion of myth and history, in which the real facts are disengaged only by conjecture.

The prehistoric Sumerian dynasties were all transformed into the realm of myth and legend. Nevertheless, these rulers, although appearing in the pretentious nomenclature as gods, appear to have been real historic personages. The name Gilgamesh was originally written *Gi-bil-aga-mis,* and means "The fire god (*Gibil*) is a commander," abbreviated to *Gi-bil-ga-mis* and *Gi(s)-bil-ga-mis,* which was finally contracted to *Gi-il-ga-mis.* Throughout the new text the name is written with the abbreviation *Gi(s)*, whereas the standard Assyrian text has consistently the writing *Gis-tu-bar*. The latter method of writing the name is apparently cryptographic for *Gis-bar-aga-(mis)*. The fire god *Gibil* has also the title *Gis-bar*.

A fragment of the South Babylonian version of the tenth book was published in 1902, a text from the period of Hammurabi, which showed that the Babylonian epic differed very much from the Assyrian in diction, but not in content. The new tablet, which belongs to the same period, also differs radically from the diction of the Ninevite text in the few lines where they duplicate each other. The first line of the new tablet corresponds to Tablet I, Col. V of the Assyrian text, where Gilgamesh begins to relate his dreams to his mother Ninsun.

The last line of Col. I corresponds to the Assyrian version Book I, Col. VI. From this point onward the new tablet takes up a hitherto unknown portion of the epic, henceforth to be assigned to the second book.

At the end of Book I in the Assyrian text, and at the end of Col. I of Book II in the new text, the situation in the legend is as follows: The harlot halts outside the city of Erech with the enamoured Enkidu while she relates to him the two dreams of the king, Gilgamesh. In these dreams, which he has told to his mother, Gilgamesh receives premonition concerning the advent of Enkidu, destined to join with him in the conquest of Elam.

Now the harlot urges Enkidu to enter the beautiful city, to clothe himself like other men and to learn the ways of civilization. When Enkidu enters he sees someone, whose name is broken away, eating bread and drinking milk, but the beautiful barbarian understands not. The harlot commands him to eat and drink also:

"It is the conformity of life,
 of the conditions and fate of the Land."

Enkidu rapidly learns the customs of men, becomes a shepherd and a mighty hunter. At last he comes to the notice of Gilgamesh himself, who is shocked by the newly acquired manner of Enkidu.

"Oh harlot, take away the man," says the Lord of Erech. Once again the faithful woman instructs her heroic lover in the conventions of society, this time teaching Enkidu the importance of the family in Babylonian life, and obedience to the ruler. Now the people of Erech assemble about Enkidu, admiring his godlike appearance. Gilgamesh receives him and they dedicate their arms to heroic endeavor. At this point the epic brings in a new and powerful *motif*, the renunciation of woman's love in the presence of a great undertaking. Gilgamesh is enamoured of the beautiful virgin goddess Ishara, and Enkidu, fearing the effeminate effects of his friend's attachment, prevents him forcibly from entering a house. A terrific combat between these two heroes ensues, in which Enkidu

conquers and, in a magnanimous speech, he reminds Gilgamesh of his higher destiny.

In another unplaced fragment of the Assyrian text, Enkidu rejects his mistress also, apparently on his own initiative and for ascetic reasons. This fragment, heretofore assigned to the second book, probably belongs to Book III. The tablet of the Assyrian version which carries the portion related on the new tablet has not been found. Man redeemed from barbarism is the major theme of Book II.

The newly recovered section of the epic contains two legends which supplied the glyptic artists of Sumer and Accad with subjects for seals. Obverse III 28-32 describes Enkidu, the slayer of lions and panthers. Seals in all periods frequently represent Enkidu in combat with a lion. The struggle between the two heroes, where Enkidu strives to rescue his friend from the fatal charms of Ishara, is probably depicted on seals also. On one of the seals published by Ward, *Seal Cylinders of Western Asia,* No. 459, a nude female stands beside the struggling heroes. This scene, not improbably, illustrates the effort of Enkidu to rescue his friend from the goddess. In fact, Enkidu stands between Gilgamesh and Ishara on the seal.

Nineveh
Christmas 1927

POSTSCRIPT

AN OLD BABYLONIAN VERSION OF THE GILGAMESH EPIC
BY
MORRIS JASTROW Jr., Ph.D., LL.D.
PROFESSOR OF SEMITIC LANGUAGES
UNIVERSITY OF PENNSYLVANIA
AND
ALBERT T. CLAY, Ph.D., LL.D., Litt.D.
PROFESSOR OF ASSYRIOLOGY AND BABYLONIAN LITERATURE
YALE UNIVERSITY
Copyright, 1920, by Yale University Press

The Gilgamesh Epic is the most notable literary product of Babylonia yet discovered in the mounds of Mesopotamia. It recounts the exploits and adventures of a favorite hero, and, in its final form, covers twelve tablets, each tablet consisting of six columns (three on the obverse and three on the reverse) of about fifty lines for each column, or a total of about 3600 lines. Of this total, however, barely more than one-half has been found among the remains of the great collection of cuneiform tablets gathered by King Ashurbanipal (668-627 B.C.) in his palace at Nineveh, and discovered by Layard in 1854 in the course of his excavations of the mound Kouyunjik (opposite Mosul). The fragments of the Epic painfully gathered—chiefly by George Smith—from the *circa* 30,000 tablets and bits of tablets brought to the British Museum were published in model form by Professor Paul Haupt, and that edition still remains the primary source for our study of the Epic.

For the sake of convenience, we may call the form of the Epic in the fragments from the library of Ashurbanipal the Assyrian version, though, like most of the literary productions in the library, it not only reverts to a Babylonian original, but represents a late copy of a much older original. The absence of any reference to Assyria in the fragments recovered justifies us in assuming that the Assyrian version received its present form in Babylonia, perhaps in Erech, though it is, of course, possible that some of the late features, particularly the elaboration of the teachings of the theologians or schoolmen in the eleventh and twelfth tablets, may have been produced at least in part under Assyrian influence. A definite indication that the Gilgamesh Epic reverts to a period earlier than Hammurabi, i.e., before 2000 B.C., was furnished by the publication of a text clearly belonging to the first Babylonian dynasty (of which Hammurabi was the sixth member) in CT. VI, 5, which text Zimmern recognized as a part of the tale of Atrahasis [Utanapishtim], one of the names given to the survivor of the deluge, recounted on the eleventh tablet of the Gilgamesh Epic. This was confirmed by the discovery of a fragment of the deluge story dated in the eleventh year of Ammisaduka, i.e., c. 1967 B.C. In this text, likewise, the name of the deluge hero appears as Atrahasis (col. VIII, 4).

But while these two tablets do not belong to the Gilgamesh Epic, and merely introduce an episode which has been incorporated into the Epic, Dr. Bruno Meissner in 1902 published a tablet, dating, as the writing and the internal evidence showed, from the Hammurabi period, which undoubtedly is a portion of what, by way of distinction, we may call an old Babylonian version. It was picked up by Dr. Meissner at a dealer's shop in Bagdad and acquired for the Berlin Museum. The tablet consists of four columns (two on the obverse and two on the reverse) and deals with the hero's wanderings in search of a cure from the disease with which he has been smitten after the death of his companion Enkidu. The hero fears that the disease will be fatal and longs to escape death. It corresponds to a portion of Tablet X of the Assyrian version. Unfortunately, only the lower portion of the obverse and the upper of the reverse have been preserved (57 lines in all), and, in default of a colophon, we do not know the numeration of the tablet in this old Babylonian edition.

Its chief value, apart from its furnishing a proof for the existence of the Epic as early as 2000 B.C., lies (a) in the writing Gish instead of Gish-gi(n)-mash in the Assyrian version for the name of the hero, (b) in the writing En-ki-du—abbreviated from dug—"Enki is good" for En-ki-doo in the Assyrian version, and (c) in the remarkable address of the maiden Sabitum [Siduri], dwelling at the seaside, to whom Gilgamesh comes in the course of his wanderings. From the Assyrian version we know that the hero tells the maiden of his grief for his lost companion, and of his longing to escape the dire fate of Enkidu. In the old Babylonian fragment, the answer of Sabitum is given in full, and the sad note that it strikes, showing how hopeless it is for man to try to escape death which is in store for all mankind, is as remarkable as is the philosophy of "eat, drink and be merry" which Sabitum imparts. The address indicates how early the tendency arose to attach to ancient tales the current religious teachings.

"Why, O Gish, does thou run about?
The life that thou seekest, thou wilt not find.
When the Gods created mankind,
Death they imposed on mankind;
Life they kept in their power.
Thou, O Gish, fill thy belly,
Day and night do thou rejoice,
Daily make a rejoicing.
Day and night a renewal of jollification.
Let thy clothes be clean,
Wash thy head and pour water over thee.
Care for the little one who takes hold of thy hand.
Let the wife rejoice in thy loins."

Such teachings, reminding us of the leading thought in the Biblical Book of Ecclesiastes, indicate the didactic character given to ancient tales that were of popular origin, but which were modified and elaborated under the influence of the schools which arose in connection with the Babylonian temples. The story itself belongs, therefore, to a still earlier period than the form it received in this old Babylonian version. The existence of this tendency at so early a date comes to us as a genuine surprise, and justifies the assumption that the attachment of a lesson to the deluge story in the Assyrian version, to wit, the limitation in attainment of immortality to those singled out by the gods as exceptions, dates likewise from the old Babylonian period. The same would apply to the twelfth tablet, which is almost entirely didactic, intended to illustrate the impossibility of learning anything of the fate of those who have passed out of this world. It also emphasizes the necessity of contenting oneself with the comfort that the care of the dead affords, by providing burial and food and drink offerings for them, as the only means of ensuring, for them, rest and freedom from the pangs of hunger and distress. However, it is of course possible that the twelfth tablet, which impresses one as a supplement to the adventures of Gilgamesh, ending with his return to Uruk (i.e., Erech) at the close of the eleventh tablet, may represent a later elaboration of the tendency to connect religious teachings with the exploits of a favorite hero.

We now have further evidence both of the extreme antiquity of the literary form of the Gilgamesh Epic and also of the disposition to make the Epic the medium of illustrating aspects of life and the destiny of mankind. The discovery by Dr. Arno Poebel of a Sumerian form of the tale of the descent of Ishtar to the lower world and her release—apparently a nature myth to illustrate the change of season from summer to winter and back again to spring—enables us to pass beyond the Akkadian (or Semitic) form of tales current in the Euphrates Valley to the

Sumerian form. Furthermore, we are indebted to Dr. Langdon for the identification of two Sumerian fragments in the Nippur Collection which deal with the adventures of Gilgamesh, one in Constantinople, and the other in the collection of the University of Pennsylvania Museum. The former, of which only twenty-five lines are preserved (nineteen on the obverse and six on the reverse), appears to be a description of the weapons of Gilgamesh with which he arms himself for an encounter—presumably the encounter with Humbaba, the ruler of the cedar forest in the mountain. The latter deals with the building operations of Gilgamesh in the city of Erech. A text in Zimmern's *Sumerische Kultlieder aus Altbabylonischer Zeit* (Leipzig, 1913), No. 196, appears likewise to be a fragment of the Sumerian version of the Gilgamesh Epic, bearing on the episode of Gilgamesh's and Enkidu's relations to the goddess Ishtar, covered in the sixth and seventh tablets of the Assyrian version.

Until, however, further fragments shall have turned up, it would be hazardous to institute a comparison between the Sumerian and the Akkadian versions. All that can be said for the present is that there is every reason to believe in the existence of a literary form of the Epic in Sumerian which presumably antedated the Akkadian recension, just as we have a Sumerian form of Ishtar's descent into the nether world, and Sumerian versions of creation myths, as also of the Deluge tale. It does not follow, however, that the Akkadian versions of the Gilgamesh Epic are translations of the Sumerian, any more than that the Akkadian creation myths are translations of a Sumerian original. Indeed, in the case of the creation myths, the striking difference between the Sumerian and Akkadian views of creation points to the independent production of creation stories on the part of the Semitic settlers of the Euphrates Valley, though no doubt these were worked out in part under Sumerian literary influences. The same is probably true of Deluge tales, which would be given a distinctly Akkadian coloring in being reproduced and steadily elaborated by the Babylonian *literati* attached to the temples.

The presumption is, therefore, in favor of an independent *literary* origin for the Semitic versions of the Gilgamesh Epic, though naturally with a duplication of the episodes, or at least of some of them, in the Sumerian narrative. Nor does the existence of a Sumerian form of the Epic necessarily prove that it originated with the Sumerians in their earliest home before they came to the Euphrates Valley. They may have adopted it after their conquest of southern Babylonia from the Semites who, there are now substantial grounds for believing, were the earlier settlers in the Euphrates Valley. We must distinguish, therefore, between the earliest *literary* form, which is undoubtedly Sumerian, and the *origin* of the episodes embodied in the Epic, including the chief actors, Gilgamesh and his companion Enkidu. It will be shown that one of the chief episodes, the encounter of the two heroes with a powerful guardian or ruler of a cedar forest, points to a

Gilgamesh

western region, more specifically to Amurru, as the scene. The names of the two chief actors, moreover, appear to have been "Sumerianized" by an artificial process and, if this view turns out to be correct, we would have a further ground for assuming the tale to have originated among the Akkadian settlers and to have been taken over from them by the Sumerians.

New light on the earliest Babylonian version of the Epic, as well as on the Assyrian version, has been shed by the recovery of two substantial fragments of the form which the Epic had assumed in Babylonia in the Hammurabi period. The study of this important new material also enables us to advance the interpretation of the Epic and to perfect the analysis into its component parts. In the spring of 1914, the Museum of the University of Pennsylvania acquired by purchase a large tablet, the writing of which, as well as the style and the manner of spelling verbal forms and substantives, pointed distinctly to the time of the first Babylonian dynasty. The tablet was identified by Dr. Arno Poebel as part of the Gilgamesh Epic and, as the colophon showed, it formed the second tablet of the series. He copied it with a view to publication, but the outbreak of war, which found him in Germany—his native country—prevented him from carrying out this intention. He, however, utilized some of its contents in his discussion of the historical or semi-historical traditions about Gilgamesh, as revealed by the important list of partly mythical and partly historical dynasties, found among the tablets of the Nippur collection, in which Gilgamesh occurs as a King of an Erech dynasty, whose father was A, a priest of Kullab.

The publication of the tablet was then undertaken by Dr. Stephen Langdon in monograph form under the title, "The Epic of Gilgamesh." In a preliminary article on the tablet in the *Museum Journal,* Vol. VIII, pages 29-38, Dr. Langdon took the tablet to be of the late Persian period (i.e., between the sixth and third century B.C.), but, his attention having been called to this error of some *1,500 years,* he corrected it in his introduction to his edition of the text, though he neglected to change some of his notes in which he still refers to the text as "late." In addition to a copy of the text, accompanied by a good photograph, Dr. Langdon furnished a transliteration and translation with some notes and a brief introduction. The text is, unfortunately, badly copied, being full of errors, and the translation is likewise very defective. A careful collation with the original tablet was made with the assistance of Dr. Edward Chiera, and, as a consequence, we are in a position to offer to scholars a correct text.

We beg to acknowledge our obligations to Dr. Gordon, the Director of the Museum of the University of Pennsylvania, for kindly placing the tablet at our disposal. While credit should be given to Dr. Langdon for having made this important tablet accessible, the interests of science demand that attention be called to his failure to grasp the many important data furnished by the tablet, which escaped him because of his erroneous readings and faulty translations.

The tablet, consisting of six columns (three on the obverse and three on the reverse), comprised, according to the colophon, 240 lines and formed the second tablet of the series. Of the total, 204 lines are preserved in full or in part, and, of the missing thirty-six, quite a number can be restored, so that we have a fairly complete tablet. The most serious break occurs at the top of the reverse, where about eight lines are missing. In consequence of this, the connection between the end of the obverse (where about five lines are missing) and the beginning of the reverse is obscured, though not to the extent of our entirely losing the thread of the narrative.

About the same time that the University of Pennsylvania Museum purchased this second tablet of the Gilgamesh Series, Yale University obtained a tablet from the same dealer, which turned out to be a continuation of the University of Pennsylvania tablet. That the two belong to the same edition of the Epic is shown by their agreement in the dark brown color of the clay, in the writing, as well as in the size of the tablet, though the characters on the Yale tablet are somewhat cramped and, in consequence, more difficult to read. Both tablets consist of six columns, three on the obverse and three on the reverse. The measurements of both are about the same, the Pennsylvania tablet being estimated at about 7 inches high, as against 7 1/8 inches for the Yale tablet, while the width of both is 6 ½ inches. The Yale tablet is, however, more closely written and therefore has a larger number of lines than the Pennsylvania tablet.

The colophon to the Yale tablet is unfortunately missing, but from internal evidence it is quite certain that the Yale tablet follows immediately upon the Pennsylvania tablet and, therefore, may be set down as the third of the series. The obverse is very badly preserved, so that only a general view of its contents can be secured. The reverse contains serious gaps in the first and second columns. The scribe evidently had a copy before him which he tried to follow exactly, but finding that he could not get all of the copy before him in the six columns, he continued the last column on the edge. In this way, we obtain for the sixth column 64 lines as against 45 for column IV, and 47 for column V, and a total of 292 lines for the six columns. Subtracting the 16 lines written on the edge leaves us 276 lines for our tablet as against 240 for its companion. The width of each column being the same on both tablets, the difference of 36 lines is made up by the closer writing.

Coming to the contents of the two tablets, the Pennsylvania tablet deals with the meeting of the two heroes, Gilgamesh and Enkidu, their conflict, followed by their reconciliation, while the Yale tablet, in continuation, takes up the preparations for the encounter of the two heroes with the guardian of the cedar forest, Humbaba—but probably pronounced Hubaba—or, as the name appears in the old

Babylonian version, Huwawa. The two tablets correspond, therefore, to portions of Tablets I to V of the Assyrian version, but, as will be shown in detail further on, the number of *completely* parallel passages is not large, and the Assyrian version shows an independence of the old Babylonian version that is larger than we had reason to expect. In general, it may be said that the Assyrian version is more elaborate, which points to its having received its present form at a considerably later period than the old Babylonian version. On the other hand, we already find in the Babylonian version the tendency toward repetition, which is characteristic of Babylonian-Assyrian tales in general. Through the two Babylonian tablets we are enabled to fill out certain details of the two episodes with which they deal: (1) the meeting of Gilgamesh and Enkidu, and (2) the encounter with Humbaba, while their greatest value consists in the light that they throw on the gradual growth of the Epic until it reached its definite form in the text represented by the fragments in Ashurbanipal's Library.

Let us now take up the detailed analysis, first of the Pennsylvania tablet and then of the Yale tablet. The Pennsylvania tablet begins with the two dreams recounted by Gilgamesh to his mother, which the latter interprets as presaging the coming of Enkidu to Erech. In the one, something like a heavy meteor falls from heaven upon Gilgamesh and almost crushes him. With the help of the heroes of Erech, Gilgamesh carries the heavy burden to his mother Ninsun. The burden, his mother explains, symbolizes someone who, like Gilgamesh, is born in the mountains, to whom all will pay homage, and of whom Gilgamesh will become enamoured with a love as strong as that for a woman. In a second dream, Gilgamesh sees someone who is like him, who brandishes an axe, and with whom he falls in love. This personage, his mother explains, is again Enkidu.

Langdon is of the opinion that these dreams are recounted to Enkidu by a woman with whom Enkidu cohabits for six days and seven nights and who weans Enkidu from association with animals. This, however, cannot be correct. The scene between Enkidu and the woman must have been recounted in detail in the first tablet, as in the Assyrian version, whereas here in the second tablet we have the continuation of the tale with Gilgamesh recounting his dreams directly to his mother. The story then continues with the description of the coming of Enkidu, conducted by the woman to the outskirts of Erech, where food is given him. The main feature of the incident is the conversion of Enkidu to civilized life. Enkidu, who hitherto had gone about naked, is clothed by the woman. Instead of sucking milk and drinking from a trough like an animal, food and strong drink are placed before him, and he is taught how to eat and drink in human fashion. In human fashion he also becomes drunk, and his "spree" is naively described: "His heart became glad and his face shone." Like an animal, Enkidu's body had hitherto been covered with hair, which is now shaved off. He is anointed with oil, and clothed "like a man." Enkidu becomes a shepherd, protecting the fold against wild beasts, and his exploit in dispatching lions is briefly told.

At this point—the end of column 3 (on the obverse), i.e., line 117, and the beginning of column 4 (on the reverse), i.e., line 131—a gap of 13 lines—the tablet is obscure, but apparently the story of Enkidu's gradual transformation from savagery to civilized life is continued, with stress upon his introduction to domestic ways with the wife chosen or decreed for him, and with work as part of his fate. All this has no connection with Gilgamesh, and it is evident that the tale of Enkidu was originally an *independent* tale to illustrate the evolution of man's career and destiny, how through intercourse with a woman he awakens to the sense of human dignity, how he becomes accustomed to the ways of civilization, how he passes through the pastoral stage to higher walks of life, how the family is instituted, and how men come to be engaged in the labors associated with human activities.

In order to connect this tale with the Gilgamesh story, the two heroes are brought together; the woman taking on herself, in addition to the role of civilizer, that of the medium through which Enkidu is brought to Gilgamesh. The woman leads Enkidu from the outskirts of Erech into the city itself, where the people on seeing him remark upon his likeness to Gilgamesh. He is the very counterpart of the latter, though somewhat smaller in stature. There follows the encounter between the two heroes in the streets of Erech, where they engage in a fierce combat. The tablet closes with the endeavor of Enkidu to pacify Gilgamesh. Enkidu declares that the mother of Gilgamesh has exalted her son above the ordinary mortal, and that Enlil himself has singled him out for royal prerogatives.

After this, we may assume, the two heroes become friends and together proceed to carry out certain exploits, the first of which is an attack upon the mighty guardian of the cedar forest. This is the main episode in the Yale tablet, which, therefore, forms the third tablet of the old Babylonian version.

In the first column of the obverse of the Yale tablet, which is badly preserved, it would appear that the elders of Erech (or perhaps the people) are endeavoring to dissuade Gilgamesh from making the attempt to penetrate to the abode of Humbaba. If this is correct, then the close of the first column may represent a conversation between these elders and the woman who accompanies Enkidu. It would be the elders who are represented as "reporting the speech to the woman," which is presumably the determination of Gilgamesh to fight Humbaba. The elders apparently desire Enkidu to accompany Gilgamesh in this perilous adventure, and, with this in view, appeal to the woman. In the second column, after an obscure reference to the mother of Gilgamesh—perhaps appealing to the sun-god—we find Gilgamesh and Enkidu again face to face. From the reference to Enkidu's eyes "filled with tears," we may conclude that he is moved to pity at the thought of what will happen to Gilgamesh if he insists upon carrying out his purpose. Enkidu also tries to dissuade Gilgamesh. This appears to be the main purport of the dialog between the two, which begins about the middle of the second column and extends to the end of the third column. Enkidu pleads that even his strength is insufficient,

"My arms are lame.
My strength has become weak." (lines 88-89)

Gilgamesh apparently asks for a description of the terrible tyrant who thus arouses the fear of Enkidu, and, in reply, Enkidu tells him how, at one time, when he was roaming about with the cattle, he penetrated into the forest and heard the roar of Humbaba, which was like that of a deluge. The mouth of the tyrant emitted fire, and his breath was death. It is clear, as Professor Haupt has suggested, that Enkidu furnishes the description of a volcano in eruption, with its mighty roar, spitting forth fire and belching out a suffocating smoke. Gilgamesh is, however, undaunted and urges Enkidu to accompany him in the adventure.

"I will go down to the forest," says Gilgamesh, if the conjectural restoration of the line in question (l. 126) is correct. Enkidu replies by again drawing a lurid picture of what will happen "When we go (together) to the forest...." This speech of Enkidu is continued on the reverse. In reply, Gilgamesh emphasizes his reliance upon the good will of Shamash, and reproaches Enkidu for cowardice. He declares himself superior to Enkidu's warning and, in bold terms, says that he prefers to perish in the attempt to overcome Humbaba, rather than abandon it.

"Wherever terror is to be faced,
Thou, forsooth, art in fear of death.
Thy prowess lacks strength.
I will go before thee,
Though thy mouth shouts to me: 'thou art afraid to approach,'
If I fall, I will establish my name." (lines 143-148)

There follows an interesting description of the forging of the weapons for the two heroes in preparation for the encounter. The elders of Erech, when they see these preparations, are stricken with fear. They learn of Humbaba's threat to annihilate Gilgamesh if he dares to enter the cedar forest, and once more try to dissuade Gilgamesh from the undertaking.

"Thou art young, O Gish, and thy heart carries thee away.
Thou dost not know what thou proposest to do." (lines 190-191)

They try to frighten Gilgamesh by repeating the description of the terrible Humbaba. Gilgamesh is still undaunted and prays to his patron deity Shamash, who apparently accords him a favorable "oracle" (*tertu*). The two heroes arm themselves for the fray, and the elders of Erech, now reconciled to the perilous undertaking, counsel Gilgamesh to take provision along for the journey. They urge Gilgamesh to allow Enkidu to take the lead, for,

"He is acquainted with the way, he has trodden the road
(to) the entrance of the forest." (lines 252-253)

The elders dismiss Gilgamesh with fervent wishes that Enkidu may track out the "closed path" for Gilgamesh, and commit him to the care of Lugalbanda—here perhaps an epithet of Shamash. They advise Gilgamesh to perform certain rites, to wash his feet in the stream of Humbaba and to pour out a libation of water to Shamash. Enkidu follows in a speech likewise intended to encourage the hero, and, with the actual beginning of the expedition against Humbaba, the tablet ends. The encounter, itself, with the triumph of the two heroes, must have been described in the fourth tablet.

Now, before taking up the significance of the additions to our knowledge of the Epic gained through these two tablets, it will be well to discuss the forms in which the names of the two heroes and of the ruler of the cedar forest occur in our tablets.

As in the Meissner fragment, the chief hero is invariably designated as Gish in both the Pennsylvania and Yale tablets, and we may therefore conclude that this was the common form in the Hammurabi period, as against the writing Gish-gi(n)-mash in the Assyrian version. Similarly, as in the Meissner fragment, the second hero's name is always written En-ki-du (abbreviated from dug) as against En-ki-doo in the Assyrian version. Finally, we encounter in the Yale tablet for the first time the writing Hu-wa-wa as the name of the guardian of the cedar forest, as against Hum-ba-ba in the Assyrian version, though in the latter case, as we may now conclude from the Yale tablet, the name should rather be read Hu-ba-ba. The variation in the writing of the latter name is interesting as pointing to the aspirate pronunciation of the labial in both instances. The name would thus present a complete parallel to the Hebrew name Howawa (or Hobab) who appears as the brother-in-law of Moses in the P document, Numbers 10, 29. Since the name also occurs, written precisely as in the Yale tablet, among the "Amoritic" names in the important lists published by Dr. Chiera, there can be no doubt that Huwawa or Hubaba is a West Semitic name. This important fact adds to the probability that the "cedar forest" in which Huwawa dwells is none other than the Lebanon district, famed since early antiquity for its cedars. This explanation of the name Huwawa disposes of suspicions hitherto brought forward for an Elamitic origin. Gressmann still favors such an origin, though realizing that the description of the cedar forest points to the Amanus or Lebanon range. In further confirmation of the West Semitic origin of the name, we have in Lucian, *De Dea Syria*, 19, the name Kombabos (the guardian of Stratonika), which forms a perfect parallel to Hu(m)baba. Of the important bearings of this western character of the name Huwawa on the interpretation and origin of the Gilgamesh epic, suggesting that the episode of the encounter between the tyrant and the two heroes rests upon a tradition of an expedition against the West or Amurru land, we shall have more to say further on.

The variation in the writing of the name Enkidu is likewise interesting. It is evident that the form in the old Babylonian version with the sign du (i.e., dug) is the original, for it furnishes us with a suitable etymology, "Enki is good." The writing with dug, pronounced du, also shows that the sign du as the third element in the form which the name has in the Assyrian version is to be read du, and that former readings like Ea-bani must be definitely abandoned. The form with du is clearly a *phonetic* writing of the Sumerian name, the sign du being chosen to indicate the *pronunciation* (not the ideograph) of the third element dug. This is confirmed by the writing En-gi-du in the syllabary CT XVIII, 30, 10. The phonetic writing is, therefore, a warning against any endeavor to read the name by an Akkadian transliteration of the signs. This would not of itself prove that Enkidu is of Sumerian *origin*, for it might well be that the writing En-ki-du is an endeavor to give a Sumerian *aspect* to a name that may have been foreign. The element dug corresponds to the Semitic *tabu,* "good," and En-ki being originally a designation of a deity as the "lord of the land," which would be the Sumerian manner of indicating a Semitic Baal, it is not at all impossible that En-ki-dug may well be the "Sumerianized" form of a Semitic "Baal is good."

It will be recalled that in the third column of the Yale tablet, Enkidu speaks of himself in his earlier period, while still living with cattle, as wandering into the cedar forest of Huwawa, while, in another passage (ll. 252-253), he is described as "acquainted with the way…to the entrance of the forest." This would clearly point to the West as the original home of Enkidu. We are thus led once more to Amurru —taken as a general designation of the West—as playing an important role in the Gilgamesh Epic. If Gilgamesh's expedition against Huwawa of the Lebanon district recalls a Babylonian campaign against Amurru, Enkidu's coming from his home, where, as we read repeatedly in the Assyrian version,

"He ate herbs with the gazelles,
Drank out of a trough with cattle,"

may rest on a tradition of an Amorite invasion of Babylonia. The fight between Gilgamesh and Enkidu would fit in with this tradition, while the subsequent reconciliation would be the form in which the tradition would represent the enforced union between the invaders and the older settlers.

Leaving this aside for the present, let us proceed to a consideration of the relationship of the form Gish, for the chief personage in the Epic in the old Babylonian version, to Gish-gi(n)-mash in the Assyrian version. Of the meaning of Gish there is, fortunately, no doubt. It is clearly the equivalent to the Akkadian *zikaru,* "man" (Brunnow No. 5707), or possibly *rabu,* "great" (Brunnow No. 5704). Among various equivalents, the preference is to be given to *itlu,* "hero."

The determinative for deity stamps the person so designated as deified, or as in part divine, and this is in accord with the express statement in the Assyrian version of the Gilgamesh Epic which describes the hero as,

"Two-thirds god and one-third human."

Gish is, therefore, our hero-god *par excellence*; and this shows that we are not dealing with a genuine proper name, but rather with a descriptive attribute. Proper names are not formed in this way, either in Sumerian or Akkadian. Now, what relation does this form Gish bear to Gish-gi(n)-mash, as the name of the hero is invariably written in the Assyrian version, the form of which was at first read Iz-tu-bar or Gish-du-bar by scholars, until Pinches found, in a neo-Babylonian syllabary, the equation of it with Gi-il-ga-mesh? Pinches' discovery pointed conclusively to the popular pronunciation of the hero's name as Gilgamesh; and, since Aelian *(De Natura Animalium* XII, 2) mentions a Babylonian personage Gilgamos (though what he tells us of Gilgamos does not appear in our Epic, but seems to apply to Etana, another figure of Babylonian mythology), there seemed to be no further reason to question that the problem had been solved. Besides, in a later Syriac list of Babylonian kings found in the Scholia of Theodor bar Koni, the name Gilgamos occurs, and it is evident that we have here again the Gil-ga-mesh discovered by Pinches. The existence of an old Babylonian hero Gilgamesh, who was likewise a king, is thus established.

It is evident that we cannot read this name as Iz-tu-bar or Gish-du-bar, but that we must read the first sign as Gish and the third as Mash, while for the second we must assume a reading Gin or Gi. This would give us Gish-gi(n)-mash, which is clearly again (like En-ki-du) not an etymological writing, but a *phonetic* one, intended to convey an *approach* to the popular pronunciation. Gi-il-ga-mesh might well be merely a variant for Gish-ga-mesh, or vice versa, and this would come close to Gish-gi-mash.

Now, when we have a name, the pronunciation of which is not definite but approximate, and which is written in various ways, the probabilities are that the name is foreign. A foreign name might naturally be spelled in various ways. The Epic in the Assyrian version clearly depicts Gish-gi(n)-mash as a conqueror of Erech, who forces the people into subjection, and whose autocratic rule leads the people of Erech to implore the goddess Aruru to create a rival to him who may withstand him. In response to this appeal, Enkidu is formed out of dust by Aruru and eventually brought to Erech. Gish-gi(n)-mash or Gilgamesh is therefore in all probability a foreigner; and the simplest solution suggested by the existence of the two forms (1) Gish, in the old Babylonian version, and (2) Gish-gi(n)-mash, in the Assyrian version, is to regard the former as an abbreviation, which seemed appropriate, because the short name conveyed the idea of the "hero" *par excellence*. If Gish-gi(n)-mash is a foreign name, one would think in the first instance of Sumerian. But here we encounter a difficulty in the circumstance that, outside of the Epic, this conqueror and ruler of Erech appears in quite a different form, namely, as Gish-bil-ga-mesh, with Gish-gibil-ga-mesh and Gish-bil-ge-mesh as variants.

In the remarkable list of partly mythological and partly historical dynasties, published by Poebel, the fifth member of the first dynasty of Erech appears as Gish-bil-ga-mesh, and, similarly, in an inscription of the days of Sin-gamil, Gish-bil-ga-mesh is mentioned as the builder of the wall of Erech. Moreover, in the several fragments of the Sumerian version of the Epic, we invariably have the form Gish-bil-ga-mesh. It is evident, therefore, that this is the genuine form of the name in Sumerian and presumably, therefore, the oldest form. By way of further confirmation, we have, in the syllabary above referred to, CT, XVIII, 30, 6-8, three designations of our hero, viz:

Gish-gibil(or bil)-ga-mesh
Muk-tab-lu ("warrior")
A-lik-pa-na ("leader")

All three designations are set down as the equivalent of the Sumerian Esigga Imin, i.e., "the seven-fold hero." Of the same general character is the equation in another syllabary: Esigga-tuk and its equivalent Gish-tuk ("the one who is a hero.") Furthermore, the name occurs frequently in "Temple" documents of the Ur dynasty in the form Gish-bil-ga-mesh, with Gish-bil-gi(n)-mesh as a variant. In a list of deities (CT XXV, 28, K 7659) we likewise encounter Gish-gibil(or bil)-ga-mesh and, lastly, in a syllabary, we have the equation Gish-gi-mas-[si?] = Gish-bil-[ga-mesh].

The variant Gish-gibil for Gish-bil may be disposed of readily, in view of the frequent confusion or interchange of the two signs Bil (Brunnow no. 4566) and Gibil (Brunnow no. 4642), which has also the value Gi (Brunnow No. 4641), so that we might also read Gish-gi-ga-mesh. Both signs convey the idea of "fire," "renew," etc.; both revert to the picture of flames of fire, in the one case with a bowl (or some such object) above it, in the other the flames issuing apparently from a torch. The meaning of the name is not affected whether we read Gish-bil-ga-mesh or Gish-gibil-ga-mesh, for the middle element in the latter case being identical with the fire-god, written Bil-gi, and to be pronounced in the inverted form as Gibil, with –ga (or ge) as the phonetic complement. It is equivalent, therefore, to the writing bil-ga in the former case. Now Gish-gibil or Gish-bil conveys the idea of *abu,* "father" (Brunnow No. 5713), just as Bil (Brunnow No. 4579) has this meaning, while Pa-gibil-(ga) or Pa-bil-ga is *abu abi,* "grandfather." This meaning may be derived from Gibil, as also from Bil = *isatu,* "fire," then *essu,* "new," then *abu,* "father," as the renewer or creator. Gish with Bil or Gibil would, therefore, be "the father-man" or "the father-hero," i.e., again the hero *par excellence,* the original hero, just as in Hebrew and Arabic *ab* is used in this way. The syllable *ga* being a phonetic complement, the element *mesh* is to be taken by itself and to be explained, as Poebel suggested, as "hero" (*itlu*, Brunnow No. 5967).

We would thus obtain an entirely artificial combination, "man (or hero), father, hero," which would simply convey, in an emphatic manner, the idea of the *Ur-held*, the original hero, the father of heroes as it were—practically the same idea, therefore, as the one conveyed by Gish alone, as the hero *par excellence.* Our investigation thus leads us to a substantial identity between Gish and the longer form Gish-bil-ga-mesh, and the former might, therefore, well be used as an abbreviation of the latter. Both the shorter and the longer forms are *descriptive epithets* based on naïve folk etymology, rather than personal names, just as in the designation of our hero as *muktablu*, "the fighter," or as *alik pana*, "the leader," or as *Esigga Imin*, "the seven-fold hero," or *Esigga Tuk*, "the one who is a hero," are descriptive epithets, and as *Atrahasis*, "the very wise one," is such an epithet for the hero of the deluge story.

The case is different with Gi-il-ga-mesh, or Gish-gi(n)-mash, which represent the popular and actual pronunciation of the name, or at least the *approach* to such pronunciation. Such forms, stripped as they are of all artificiality, impress one as genuine names. The conclusion to which we are thus led is that Gish-bil-ga-mesh is a play upon the genuine name, to convey to those to whom the real name, as that of a foreigner, would suggest no meaning as an interpretation *fitting in with his character*. In other words, Gish-bil-ga-mesh is a "Sumerianized" form of the name, introduced into the Sumerian version of the tale which became a folk-possession in the Euphrates valley. Such plays upon names to suggest the character of an individual or some incident are familiar to us from the narratives in Genesis. They do not constitute genuine etymologies, and are rarely of use in leading to a correct etymology. Reuben, e.g., certainly does not mean "Yahweh has seen my affliction," which the mother is supposed to have exclaimed at the birth (Genesis 29, 32), with a play upon *ben* and *be'onyi*, any more than Judah means "I praise Yahweh" (v. 35), though it does contain the divine name (*Yeho*) as an element. The play on the name may be close or remote, as long as it fulfills its function of *suggesting* an etymology that is complimentary or appropriate.

In this way, an artificial division and, at the same time, a distortion of a foreign name like Gilgamesh into several elements, Gish-bil-ga-mesh, is no more violent than, for example, the explanation of Issachar, or rather Issaschar, as "God has given my hire" (Genesis 30, 18) with a play upon the element *sechar*, and as though the name were to be divided into *Yah* ("God") and *sechar* ("hire"); or the popular name of Alexander among the Arabs as *Zu'l Karnaini*, "the possessor of the two horns," with a suggestion of his conquest of two hemispheres.

The element Gil in Gilgamesh would be regarded as a contraction of Gish-bil or gi-bil, in order to furnish the meaning "father-hero," or Gil might be looked upon as a variant for Gish, which would give us the "phonetic" form in the Assyrian version Gish-gi-mash, as well as such a variant writing Gish-gi-mas-(si). Now a name like Gilgamesh, upon which we may definitely settle as coming closest to the genuine form, certainly impresses one as foreign, i.e., it is neither Sumerian nor Akkadian; and we have already suggested that the circumstance that the hero of the Epic is portrayed as a conqueror of Erech, and a rather ruthless one at that, points to a tradition of an invasion of the Euphrates valley as the background for the episode in the first tablet of the series.

Now it is significant that many of the names in the "mythical" dynasties, as they appear in Poebel's list, are likewise foreign, such as Mes-ki-in-ga-se-ir, son of the god Shamash (and the founder of the "mythical" dynasty of Erech of which Gish-bil-ga-mesh is the fifth member), and En-me-ir-kar, his son. In a still earlier "mythical" dynasty, we encounter names like Ga-lu-mu-um, Zu-ga-gi-ib, Ar-pi, E-ta-na, which are distinctly foreign, while such names as En-me(n)-nun-na and Bar-sal-nun-na strike one again as "Sumerianized" names, rather than as genuine Sumerian formations.

Some of these names, such as Galumum, Arpi and Etana, are so Amoritic in appearance that one may hazard the conjecture of their western origin. May Gilgamesh likewise belong to the Amurru region, or does he represent a foreigner from the East in contrast to Enkidu, whose name, we have seen, may have been Baal-Tob in the West, with which region he is, according to the Epic, so familiar? It must be confessed that the second element, *ga-mesh,* would fit in well with a Semitic origin for the name, for the element impresses one as the participial form of a Semitic stem g-m-s, just as in the second element of Meskin-gaser we have such a form. Gil might then be the name of a West-Semitic deity. Such conjectures, however, can for the present not be substantiated, and we must content ourselves with the conclusion that Gilgamesh, as the real name of the hero, or at least the form which comes closest to the real name, points to a foreign origin for the hero, and that such forms as Gish-bil-ga-mesh and Gish-bil-gi-mesh and other variants are "Sumerianized" forms for which an artificial etymology was brought forward to convey the idea of the "original hero" or the hero *par excellence.*

By means of this "play" on the name, which reverts to the compilers of the Sumerian version of the Epic, Gilgamesh was converted into a Sumerian figure, just as the name Enkidu may have been introduced as a Sumerian translation of his Amoritic name. Gish, at all events, is an abbreviated form of the "Sumerianized" name, introduced by the compilers of the earliest Akkadian version, which was produced naturally under the influence of the Sumerian version. Later, as the Epic continued to grow, a phonetic writing was introduced, Gish-gi-mash, which is in a measure a compromise between the genuine name and the "Sumerianized" form, but, at the same time, an *approach* to the real pronunciation.

Next, to the new light thrown upon the names and original character of the two main figures of the Epic, one of the chief points of interest in the Pennsylvania fragment is the proof that it furnishes for a striking resemblance of the two heroes, Gish and Enkidu, to one another. In interpreting the dream of Gish, his mother, Ninsun, lays stress upon the fact that the dream portends the coming of someone who is like Gish, "born in the field and reared in the mountain" (lines 18-19). Both, therefore, are shown by this description to have come to Babylonia from a mountainous region, i.e., they are foreigners. And, in the case of Enkidu, we have seen that the mountain, in all probability, refers to a region in the West, while the same may also be the case with Gish. The resemblance of the two heroes to one another extends to their personal appearance. When Enkidu appears on the streets of Erech, the people are struck by this resemblance. They remark that he is "like Gish," though "shorter in stature" (lines 179-180). Enkidu is described as a rival or counterpart.

This relationship between the two is suggested also by the Assyrian version. In the creation of Enkidu by Aruru, the people urge the goddess to create the "counterpart" (*zikru*) of Gilgamesh, someone who will be like him (*ma-si-il*) (Tablet I, 2, 31). Enkidu not only comes from the mountain, but the mountain is specifically designated as his birth-place (I, 4, 2), precisely as in the Pennsylvania tablet, while, in another passage, he is also described, as in our tablet, as "born in the field." Still more significant is the designation of Gilgamesh as the *talimu*, "younger brother," of Enkidu. In accord with this, we find Gilgamesh in his lament over Enkidu describing him as a "younger brother" *(ku-ta-ni)*. And again, in the last tablet of the Epic, Gilgamesh is referred to as the "brother" of Enkidu. This close relationship reverts to the Sumerian version, for the Constantinople fragment (Langdon, above, p. 13) begins with the designation of Gish-bil-ga-mesh as "his brother." By "his" no doubt Enkidu is meant. Likewise, in the Sumerian text published by Zimmern (above, p.13), Gilgamesh appears as the brother of Enkidu (rev. 1, 17).

Turning to the numerous representations of Gilgamesh and Enkidu on Seal Cylinders, we find this resemblance of the two heroes to each other strikingly confirmed. Both are represented as bearded, with the strands arranged in the same fashion. The face in both cases is broad, with curls protruding at the side of the head, though, at times, these curls are lacking in the case of Enkidu. What is particularly striking is to find Gilgamesh generally *a little taller* than Enkidu, thus bearing out the statement in the Pennsylvania tablet that Enkidu is "shorter in stature." There are, to be sure, also some distinguishing marks between the two. Thus Enkidu is generally represented with animal hoofs, but not always. Enkidu is commonly portrayed with the horns of a bison, but again this sign is wanting in quite a number of instances. The hoofs and horns mark the period when Enkidu lived with animals and much like an animal. Most remarkable, however, of all are cylinders on which we find the two heroes almost exactly alike as, for example, Ward No. 199, where the two figures, the one a duplicate of the other (except that one is just a shade taller), are in conflict with each other. Dr. Ward was puzzled by this representation and sets it down as a "fantastic" scene in which "each Gilgamesh is stabbing the other." In the light of the Pennsylvania tablet, this scene is clearly the conflict between the two heroes described in column 6, preliminary to their forming a friendship. Even in the realm of myth, the human experience holds true that there is nothing like a good fight as the basis for a subsequent alliance. The fragment describes this conflict as a furious one in which Gilgamesh is worsted, and his wounded pride assuaged by the generous victor, who comforts his vanquished enemy by the assurance that he was destined for something higher than to be a mere "Hercules." He was singled out for the exercise of royal authority.

True to the description of the two heroes in the Pennsylvania tablet as alike, one the counterpart of the other, the seal cylinder portrays them almost exactly alike, as alike as two brothers could possibly be, with just enough distinction to make it clear on close inspection that two figures are intended, and not one repeated for the sake of symmetry. There are slight variations in the manner in which the hair is worn, and slightly varying expressions of the face, just enough to make it evident that the one is intended for Gilgamesh and the other for Enkidu. When, therefore, in another specimen, No. 173, we find a Gilgamesh holding his counterpart by the legs, it is merely another aspect of the fight between the two heroes, one of whom is intended to represent Enkidu, and not, as Dr. Ward supposed, a grotesque repetition of Gilgamesh.

The description of Enkidu in the Pennsylvania tablet as a parallel figure to Gilgamesh leads us to a consideration of the relationship of the two figures to one another. Many years ago it was pointed out that the Gilgamesh Epic was a composite tale in which various stories of an independent origin had been combined and brought into more or less artificial connection with the *heros eponymos* of southern Babylonia. We may now go a step further and point out that not only is Enkidu originally an entirely independent figure, having no connection with Gish or Gilgamesh, but that the latter is really depicted in the Epic as the counterpart of Enkidu, a reflection who has been given the traits of extraordinary physical power that belong to Enkidu. This is shown in the first place by the fact that in the encounter it is Enkidu who triumphs over Gilgamesh. [This interpretation has been questioned by the discovery of later fragments and tablets.] The entire analysis of the episode of the meeting between the two heroes as given by Gressmann must be revised. It is not Enkidu who is terrified and who is warned against the encounter. It is Gilgamesh who, during the night on his way from the house in which the goddess Ishara lies, encounters Enkidu on the highway. Enkidu "blocks the path" of Gilgamesh. He prevents Gilgamesh from re-entering the house and the two attack each other "like oxen." They grapple with each other and Enkidu forces Gilgamesh to the ground. Enkidu is, therefore, the real hero whose traits of physical prowess are afterwards transferred to Gilgamesh.

Similarly, in the next episode, the struggle against Huwawa, the Yale tablet makes it clear that, in the original form of the tale, Enkidu is the real hero. All warn Gish against the undertaking—the elders of Erech, Enkidu, and also the workmen. "Why dost thou desire to do this?" they say to him. "Thou art young, and thy heart carries thee away. Thou knowest not what thou proposest to do." This part of the incident is now better known to us through the latest fragment of the Assyrian version discovered and published by King. The elders say to Gilgamesh,

"Do not trust, O Gilgamesh, in thy strength.
Be warned(?) against trusting to thy attack.
The one who goes before will save his companion,
He who has foresight will save his friend.
Let Enkidu go before thee.
He knows the roads to the cedar forest;
He is skilled in battle and has seen combat."

Gilgamesh is sufficiently impressed by this warning to invite Enkidu to accompany him on a visit to his mother, Ninsun, for the purpose of receiving her counsel.

It is only after Enkidu, who himself hesitates and tries to dissuade Gish, decides to accompany the latter that the elders of Erech are reconciled and encourage Gish for the fray. The two in concert proceed against Huwawa. Gilgamesh alone cannot carry out the plan. Now, when a tale thus associates two figures in one deed, one of the two has been added to the original tale. In the present case, there can be little doubt that Enkidu, without whom Gish cannot proceed, who is specifically described as "acquainted with the way to the entrance of the forest" in which Huwawa dwells, is the *original* vanquisher. Naturally, the Epic aims to conceal this fact as much as possible *ad majorem gloriam* of Gilgamesh. It tries to put the one who became the favorite hero into the foreground. Therefore, in both the Babylonian and the Assyrian version, Enkidu is represented as hesitating, and Gilgamesh as determined to go ahead. Gilgamesh, in fact, accuses Enkidu of cowardice and boldly declares that he will proceed even though failure may stare him in the face. Traces of the older view, however, in which Gilgamesh is the one for whom one fears the outcome, crop out; as, for example, in the complaint of Gilgamesh's mother to Shamash that the latter has stirred the heart of her son to take the distant way to Hu(m)baba,

"To a fight unknown to him, he advances,
An expedition unknown to him, he undertakes."

Ninsun evidently fears the consequences when her son informs her of his intention and asks her counsel. The answer of Shamash is not preserved, but no doubt it was of a reassuring character, as was the answer of the Sun-God to Gish's appeal and prayer as set forth in the Yale tablet.

Again, as a further indication that Enkidu is the real conqueror of Huwawa, we find the coming contest revealed to Enkidu no less than three times in dreams, which Gilgamesh interprets. [This interpretation has been questioned by the discovery of later fragments and tablets.] Since the person who dreams is always the one to whom the dream applies, we may see in these dreams a further trace of the primary role originally assigned to Enkidu.

Another exploit which, according to the Assyrian version, the two heroes perform in concert is the killing of a bull, sent by Anu at the instance of Ishtar to avenge an insult offered to the goddess by Gilgamesh, who rejects her offer of marriage. In the fragmentary description of the contest with the bull, we find Enkidu "seizing" the monster by "its tail."

That Enkidu originally played the part of the slayer is also shown by the statement that it is he who insults Ishtar by throwing a piece of the carcass into the goddess' face, adding also an insulting speech; and this despite the fact that Ishtar, in her rage, accuses Gilgamesh of killing the bull. It is thus evident that the Epic alters the original character of the episodes in order to find a place for Gilgamesh, with the further desire to assign to the latter the *chief* role. Be it noted also that Enkidu, not Gilgamesh, is punished for the insult to Ishtar. Enkidu must, therefore, in the original form of the episode, have been the guilty party who is stricken with mortal disease as a punishment to which, after twelve days, he succumbs. In view of this, we may supply the name of Enkidu in the little song introduced at the close of the encounter with the bull, and not Gilgamesh, as has hitherto been done.

"Who is distinguished among heroes?
Who is glorious among men?
[Enkidu] is distinguished among heroes,
[Enkidu] is glorious among men."

Finally, the killing of lions is directly ascribed to Enkidu in the Pennsylvania tablet:

"Lions he attacked
Lions he overcame"

whereas Gilgamesh appears to be afraid of lions. On his long search for Utanapishtim, Gilgamesh says:

"On reaching the entrance of the mountain at night
I saw lions and was afraid."

Gilgamesh prays to Sin and Ishtar to protect and save him. When, therefore, in another passage, someone celebrates Gilgamesh as the one who overcame the "guardian," who dispatched Hu(m)baba in the cedar forest, who killed lions and overthrew the bull, we have the completion of the process which transferred to Gilgamesh exploits and powers which originally belonged to Enkidu, though ordinarily the process stops short at making Gilgamesh a *sharer* in the exploits, with the natural tendency, to be sure, to enlarge the share of the favorite.

We can now understand why the two heroes are described in the Pennsylvania tablet as alike, as born in the same place, aye, as brothers. Gilgamesh in the Epic is merely a reflex of Enkidu. The latter is the real hero and, presumably, therefore, the older figure. Gilgamesh resembles Enkidu, because he *is* originally Enkidu. The "resemblance" motif is merely the manner in which, in the course of the partly popular, partly literary transfer, the recollection is preserved that Enkidu is the original, and Gilgamesh the copy.

The artificiality of the process which brings the two heroes together is apparent in the dreams of Gilgamesh which are interpreted by his mother as portending the coming of Enkidu. The conflict is not foreseen, but the subsequent close association is, naively described as due to the personal charm which Enkidu exercises, which will lead Gilgamesh to fall in love with the one whom he is to meet. The two will become one, like man and wife.

On the basis of our investigations, we are now in a position to reconstruct, in part, the cycle of episodes that once formed part of an Enkidu Epic. The fight between Enkidu and Gilgamesh, in which the former is the victor, is typical of the kind of tales told of Enkidu. He is the real prototype of the Greek Hercules. He slays lions, he overcomes a powerful opponent dwelling in the forests of Lebanon, he kills the bull, and he finally succumbs to disease sent as a punishment by an angry goddess. The death of Enkidu naturally formed the close of the Enkidu Epic, which, in its original form, may of course have included other exploits besides those taken over into the Gilgamesh Epic.

There is another aspect of the figure of Enkidu which is brought forward in the Pennsylvania tablet more clearly than had hitherto been the case. Many years ago, attention was called to certain striking resemblances between Enkidu and the figure of the first man as described in the early chapters of Genesis. At that time, we had merely the Assyrian version of the Gilgamesh Epic at our disposal, and the main point of contact was the description of Enkidu living with the animals, drinking and feeding like an animal, until a woman is brought to him with whom he engages in sexual intercourse. This suggested that Enkidu was a picture of primeval man, while the woman reminded one of Eve, who, when she is brought to

Adam, becomes his helpmate and inseparable companion. The Biblical tale stands, of course, on a much higher level, and is introduced, as are other traditions and tales of primitive times, in the style of a parable to convey certain religious teachings. For all that, suggestions of earlier conceptions crop out in the picture of Adam surrounded by animals to which he assigns names. Such a phrase as "there was no helpmate corresponding to him" becomes intelligible on the supposition of an existing tradition or belief that man once lived and, indeed, cohabited with animals. The tales in the early chapters of Genesis must rest on very early popular traditions, which have been cleared of mythological and other objectionable features in order to adapt them to the purpose of the Hebrew compilers, to serve as a medium for illustrating certain religious teachings regarding man's place in nature and his higher destiny. From the resemblance between Enkidu and Adam, it does not, of course, follow that the latter is modeled upon the former, but only that both rest on similar traditions of the condition under which men lived in primeval days prior to the beginnings of human culture.

We may now pass beyond these general indications and recognize in the story of Enkidu as revealed by the Pennsylvania tablet an attempt to trace the evolution of primitive man from low beginnings to the regular and orderly family life associated with advanced culture. The new tablet furnishes a further illustration for the surprisingly early tendency among the Babylonian *literati* to connect with popular tales teachings of a religious or ethical character. Just as the episode between Gilgamesh and the maiden Sabitum [Siduri] is made the occasion for introducing reflections on the inevitable fate of man to encounter death, so the meeting of Enkidu with the woman [harlot] becomes the medium of impressing the lesson of human progress through the substitution of bread and wine for milk and water, through the institution of the family, and through work and the laying up of resources.

This is the significance of the address to Enkidu in column 4 of the Pennsylvania tablet, even though certain expressions in it are somewhat obscure. The connection of the entire episode of Enkidu and the woman with Gilgamesh is very artificial, and it becomes much more intelligible if we disassociate it from its present entanglement in the Epic. In Gilgamesh's dream, portending the meeting with Enkidu, nothing is said of the woman who is the companion of the latter. The passage in which Enkidu is created by Aruru to oppose Gilgamesh betrays evidence of having been worked over in order to bring Enkidu into association with the longing of the people of Erech to get rid of a tyrannical character.

The people, in their distress, appeal to Aruru to create a rival to Gilgamesh. In response,

"Aruru, upon hearing this, created a man of Anu in her heart."

Now this "man of Anu" cannot possibly be Enkidu, for the sufficient reason that, a few lines further on, Enkidu is described as an offspring of Ninib [Ninurta]. Moreover, the being created is not a "counterpart" of Gilgamesh, but an animal-man, as the description that follows shows. We must separate lines 30-33, in which the creation of the "Anu man" is described, from lines 34-41, in which the creation of Enkidu is narrated. Indeed, these lines strike one as the proper *beginning* of the original Enkidu story, which would naturally start out with his birth and end with his death. The description is clearly an account of the creation of the first man, in which capacity Enkidu is brought forward.

"Aruru washed her hands, broke off clay,
threw it on the field
...created Enkidu, the hero, a lofty
offspring of the host of Ninib."

The description of Enkidu follows, with his body covered with hair like an animal, and eating and drinking with the animals. There follows an episode which has no connection whatsoever with the Gilgamesh Epic, but which is clearly intended to illustrate how Enkidu came to abandon the life with the animals. A hunter sees Enkidu and is amazed at the strange sight—an animal and yet a man. Enkidu, as though resenting his condition, becomes enraged at the sight of the hunter, and the latter goes to his father and tells him of the strange creature whom he is unable to catch. In reply, the father advises his son to take a woman with him when next he goes out on his pursuit, and to have the woman remove her dress in the presence of Enkidu, who will then approach her and, after intercourse with her, will abandon the animals among whom he lives. By this device he will catch the strange creature. Lines 14-18 of column 3 in the first tablet in which the father of the hunter refers to Gilgamesh must be regarded as a later insertion, a part of the reconstruction of the tale to connect the episode with Gilgamesh.

The advice of the father to his son, the hunter, begins line 19,

"Go my hunter, take with thee a woman."

In the reconstructed tale, the father tells his son to go to Gilgamesh to relate to him the strange appearance of the animal-man, but there is clearly no purpose in this, as is shown by the fact that when the hunter does so, Gilgamesh makes precisely the same speech as does the father of the hunter. Lines 40-44 of column 3, in which Gilgamesh is represented as speaking to the hunter, form a complete doublet to lines 19-24, beginning,

"Go my hunter, take with thee a woman, etc."

And similarly, the description of Enkidu appears twice, lines 2-12 in an address of the hunter to his father, and lines 29-39 in the address of the hunter to Gilgamesh.

The artificiality of the process of introducing Gilgamesh into the episode is revealed by this awkward and entirely meaningless repetition. We may therefore reconstruct the first two scenes in the Enkidu Epic as follows:

Tablet I, col. 2, 34-35: Creation of Enkidu by Aruru

36-41: Description of Enkidu's hairy body and of his life with the animals.

42-50: The hunter sees Enkidu, who shows his anger, as also his woe, at his condition.

3, 1-12: The hunter tells his father of the strange being who pulls up the traps which the hunter digs, and who tears the nets so that the hunter is unable to catch him or the animals.

19-24: The father of the hunter advises his son on his next expedition to take a woman with him in order to lure the strange being from his life with the animals.

Line 25, beginning "On the advice of his father," must have set forth, in the original form of the episode, how the hunter procured the woman and took her with him to meet Enkidu.

Column 4 gives in detail the meeting between the two and naively describes how the woman exposes her charms to Enkidu, who is captivated by her and stays with her six days and seven nights. The animals see the change in Enkidu and run away from him. He has been transformed through the woman. So far the episode. In the Assyrian version, there follows an address of the woman to Enkidu, beginning (col. 4, 34):

"Beautiful art thou, Enkidu, like a god art thou."

We find her urging him to go with her to Erech, there to meet Gilgamesh and to enjoy the pleasures of city life with plenty of beautiful maidens. Gilgamesh, she adds, will expect Enkidu, for the coming of the latter to Erech has been foretold in a dream. It is evident that here we have again the later transformation of the Enkidu Epic in order to bring the two heroes together. Will it be considered too bold if we assume that, in the original form, the address of the woman and the construction of the episode were such as we find preserved, in part, in columns 2 to 4 of the Pennsylvania tablet, which forms part of the new material that can now be added to the Epic? The address of the woman begins in line 51 of the Pennsylvania tablet:

"I gaze upon thee, Enkidu, like a god art thou."

This corresponds to the line in the Assyrian version (I, 4, 34) as given above, just as lines 52-53:

"Why with the cattle

Dost thou roam across the field?"

correspond to I, 4, 35 of the Assyrian version. There follows, in both the old Babylonian and the Assyrian version, the appeal of the woman to Enkidu, to allow her to lead him to Erech where Gilgamesh dwells (Pennsylvania tablet lines 54-

61=Assyrian version I, 4, 36-39); but, in the Pennsylvania tablet, we now have a *second* speech (lines 62-63) beginning, like the first one, with *al-ka,* "come:"

"Come, arise from the accursed ground."

Enkidu consents, and now the woman takes off her garments and clothes the naked Enkidu, while putting another garment on herself. She takes hold of his hand and leads him to the sheepfolds (not to Erech!), where bread and wine are placed before him. Accustomed, hitherto, to sucking milk with cattle, Enkidu does not know what to do with the strange food until encouraged and instructed by the woman. The entire third column is taken up with this introduction of Enkidu to civilized life in a pastoral community, and the scene ends with Enkidu becoming a guardian of flocks. Now all this has nothing to do with Gilgamesh, and clearly sets forth an entirely different idea from the one embodied in the meeting of the two heroes. In the original Enkidu tale, the animal-man is looked upon as the type of a primitive savage, and the point of the tale is to illustrate in the naïve manner characteristic of folklore the evolution to the higher form of pastoral life. This aspect of the incident is, therefore, to be separated from the other phase which has, as its chief *motif,* the bringing of the two heroes together.

We now obtain, thanks to the new section revealed by the Pennsylvania tablet, a further analogy with the story of Adam and Eve, but with this striking difference, that whereas in the Babylonian tale the woman is the medium leading man to the higher life, in the Biblical story the woman is the tempter who brings misfortune to man. This contrast is, however, not inherent in the Biblical story, but due to the point of view of the Biblical writer, who is somewhat pessimistically inclined and looks upon primitive life, when man went naked and lived in a garden, eating of fruits that grew of themselves, as the blessed life in contrast to advanced culture which leads to agriculture and necessitates hard work as the means of securing one's substance. Hence the woman through whom Adam eats of the tree of knowledge and becomes conscious of being naked is looked upon as an evil tempter, entailing the loss of the primeval life of bliss in a gorgeous Paradise. The Babylonian point of view is optimistic. The change to civilized life— involving the wearing of clothes and the eating of food that is cultivated (bread and wine) is looked upon as an advance. Hence the woman is viewed as the medium of raising man to a higher level. The feature common to the Biblical and Babylonian tales is the attachment of a lesson to early folk-tales. The story of Adam and Eve, as the story of Enkidu and the woman, is told *with a purpose.* Starting with early traditions of men's primitive life on earth that may have arisen independently, Hebrew and Babylonian writers diverged, each group going its own way, each reflecting the particular point of view from which the evolution of human society was viewed.

Leaving the analogy between the Biblical and Babylonian tales aside, the main point of value for us in the Babylonian story of Enkidu and the woman is the proof furnished by the analysis, made possible through the Pennsylvania tablet, that the tale can be separated from its subsequent connection with Gilgamesh. We can continue this process of separation in the fourth column, where the woman instructs Enkidu in the further duty of living his life with the woman decreed for him, to raise a family, to engage in work, to build cities and to gather resources. All this is looked upon in the same optimistic spirit as marking progress, whereas the Biblical writer, consistent with his point of view, looks upon work as a curse, and makes Cain, the murderer, also the founder of cities. The step to the higher forms of life is not an advance according to the J document. It is interesting to note that even the phrase "cursed ground" occurs in both the Babylonian and Biblical tales; but, whereas in the latter (Genesis 3, 17), it is because of the hard work entailed in raising the products of the earth that the ground is cursed, in the former (lines 62-63), it is the place in which Enkidu lives *before* he advances to the dignity of human life that is "cursed," and which he is asked to leave. Adam is expelled from Paradise as a punishment, whereas Enkidu is implored to leave it as a necessary step towards progress to a higher form of existence. The contrast between the Babylonian and the Biblical writer extends to the view taken of viniculture. The Biblical writer (again the J document) looks upon Noah's drunkenness as a disgrace. Noah loses his sense of shame and uncovers himself (Genesis 9, 21), whereas, in the Babylonian description, Enkidu's jolly spirit after he has drunk seven jars of wine meets with approval. The Biblical point of view is that he who drinks wine becomes drunk; the Babylonian says if you drink wine you become happy.

If the thesis here set forth of the original character and import of the episode of Enkidu with the woman is correct, we may again regard lines 149-153 of the Pennsylvania tablet, in which Gilgamesh is introduced, as a later addition to bring the two heroes into association. The episode, in its original form, ended with the introduction of Enkidu, first to pastoral life, and then to the still higher city life with regulated forms of social existence.

Now, to be sure, this Enkidu has little in common with the Enkidu who is described as a powerful warrior, a Hercules, who kills lions, overcomes the giant Huwawa, and dispatches a great bull, but it is the nature of folklore everywhere to attach to traditions about a favorite hero all kinds of tales with which originally he had nothing to do. Enkidu, as such a favorite, is viewed also as the type of primitive man, and so there arose gradually an Epic which began with his birth, pictured him as half-animal, half-man, told how he emerged from this state, how he became civilized, was clothed, learned to eat food and drink wine, how he shaved off the hair with which his body was covered, anointed himself—in short,

"He became manlike."

Thereupon, he is taught his duties as a husband, is introduced to the work of building, and to laying aside supplies, and the like. The fully-developed and full-fledged hero then engages in various exploits, of which *some* are now embodied in the Gilgamesh Epic. Who this Enkidu was, we are not in a position to determine, but the suggestion has been thrown out above that he is a personage foreign to Babylonia, that his home appears to be in the undefined Amurru district, and that he conquers that district. The original tale of Enkidu, if this view be correct, must therefore have been carried to the Euphrates valley, at a very remote period, with one of the migratory waves that brought a western people as invaders into Babylonia. Here the tale was combined with stories current of another hero, Gilgamesh—perhaps also of western origin—whose conquest of Erech likewise represents an invasion of Babylonia.

The center of the Gilgamesh tale was Erech and, in the process of combining the stories of Enkidu and Gilgamesh, Enkidu is brought to Erech and the two perform exploits in common. In such a combination, the aim would be to utilize all the incidents of *both* tales. The woman who accompanies Enkidu, therefore, becomes the medium of bringing the two heroes together. The story of the evolution of primitive man to civilized life is transformed into the tale of Enkidu's removal to Erech, and elaborated with all kinds of details, among which we have, as perhaps embodying a genuine historical tradition, the encounter of the two heroes.

Before passing on, we have merely to note the very large part taken in both the old Babylonian and the Assyrian version by the struggle against Huwawa. The entire Yale tablet—forming, as we have seen, the third of the series—is taken up with the preparation for the struggle, and with the repeated warnings given to Gilgamesh against the dangerous undertaking. The fourth tablet must have recounted the struggle itself, and it is not improbable that this episode extended into the fifth tablet, since, in the Assyrian version, this is the case. The elaboration of the story is, in itself, an argument in favor of assuming some historical background for it—the recollection of the conquest of Amurru by some powerful warrior; and we have seen that this conquest must be ascribed to Enkidu, and not to Gilgamesh.

If, now, Enkidu is not only the older figure, but the one who is the real hero of the most notable episode in the Gilgamesh Epic; if, furthermore, Enkidu is the Hercules who kills lions and dispatches the bull sent by an enraged goddess, what becomes of Gilgamesh? What is left for him?

In the first place, he is definitely the conqueror of Erech. He builds the wall of Erech, and we may assume that the designation of the city as *Uruk supuri,* "the walled Erech," rests upon this tradition. He is also associated with the great temple

Eanna, "the heavenly house," in Erech. To Gilgamesh belongs also the unenviable tradition of having exercised his rule in Erech so harshly that the people are impelled to implore Aruru to create a rival who may rid the district of the cruel tyrant, who is described as snatching sons and daughters from their families, and in other ways terrifying the population—an early example of "Schrecklichkeit." After tablets II to V, inclusive of the Assyrian version being taken up with the Huwawa episode, modified with a view of bringing the two heroes together, we come at once to the sixth tablet, which tells the story of how the goddess Ishtar wooed Gilgamesh, and of the latter's rejection of her advances. This tale is distinctly a nature myth. The attempt of Gressmann to find some historical background to the episode is a failure. The goddess Ishtar symbolizes the earth, which woos the sun in the spring, but whose love is fatal, for, after a few months, the sun's power begins to wane. Gilgamesh, who, in incantation hymns, is invoked in terms which show that he was conceived as a sun-god, recalls to the goddess how she changed her lovers into animals, like Circe of Greek mythology, and brought them to grief. Enraged at Gilgamesh's insult to her vanity, she flies to her father Anu and cries for revenge.

At this point, the episode of the creation of the bull is introduced, but, if the analysis above given is correct, it is Enkidu who is the hero in dispatching the bull, and we must assume that the sickness with which Gilgamesh is smitten is the punishment sent by Anu to avenge the insult to his daughter. This sickness symbolizes the waning strength of the sun after midsummer is past. The sun recedes from the earth, and this was pictured in the myth as the sun-god's rejection of Ishtar. Gilgamesh's fear of death marks the approach of the winter season, when the sun appears to have lost its vigor completely and is near to death. The entire episode is, therefore, a nature myth, symbolic of the passing of spring to midsummer and then to the bare season. The myth has been attached to Gilgamesh as a favorite figure, and then woven into a pattern with the episode of Enkidu and the bull. The bull episode can be detached from the nature myth without any loss to the symbolism of the tale of Ishtar and Gilgamesh.

As already suggested, with Enkidu's death after this conquest of the bull, the original Enkidu Epic came to an end. In order to connect Gilgamesh with Enkidu, the former is represented as sharing in the struggle against the bull. Enkidu is punished with death, while Gilgamesh is smitten with disease. Since both shared equally in the guilt, the punishment should have been the same for both. The differentiation may be taken as an indication that Gilgamesh's disease has nothing to do with the bull episode, but is merely part of the nature myth.

Gilgamesh now begins a series of wanderings in search of the restoration of his vigor, and this motif is evidently a continuation of the nature myth to symbolize the sun's wanderings during the dark winter in the hope of renewed vigor with the coming of the spring. Professor Haupt's view is that the disease from which Gilgamesh is supposed to be suffering is of a venereal character, affecting the organs of reproduction. This would confirm the position here taken that the myth symbolizes the loss of the sun's vigor. The sun's rays are no longer strong enough to fertilize the earth. In accord with this, Gilgamesh's search for healing leads him to the dark regions in which the scorpion-men dwell. The terrors of the region symbolize the gloom of the winter season. At last Gilgamesh reaches a region of light again, described as a landscape situated at the sea. The maiden in control of this region bolts the gate against Gilgamesh's approach, but the latter forces his entrance. It is the picture of the sun-god bursting through the darkness, to emerge as the youthful reinvigorated sun-god of the spring.

Now, with the tendency to attach to popular tales and nature myths lessons illustrative of current beliefs and aspirations, Gilgamesh's search for renewal of life is viewed as man's longing for eternal life. The sun-god's waning power after midsummer is past suggests man's growing weakness after the meridian of life has been left behind. Winter is death, and man longs to escape it. Gilgamesh's wanderings are used as illustration of this longing, and, accordingly, the search for life becomes also the quest for immortality. Can the precious boon of eternal life be achieved? Popular fancy created the figure of a favorite of the gods who had escaped a destructive deluge in which all mankind had perished. Gilgamesh hears of this favorite and determines to seek him out and learn from him the secret of eternal life.

The deluge story, again a pure nature myth, symbolical of the rainy season which destroys all life in nature, is thus attached to the Epic. Gilgamesh, after many adventures, finds himself in the presence of the survivor of the deluge who, although human, enjoys immortal life among the gods. Gilgamesh asks the survivor how he came to escape the common fate of mankind and, in reply, Utanapishtim tells the story of the catastrophe that brought about universal destruction. The moral of the tale is obvious. Only those singled out by the special favor of the gods can hope to be removed to the distant "source of the streams" and live forever. The rest of mankind must face death as the end of life.

That the story of the deluge is told in the eleventh tablet of the series, corresponding to the eleventh month, known as the month of "rain curse" and marking the height of the rainy season, may be intentional, just as it may not be accidental that Gilgamesh's rejection of Ishtar is recounted in the sixth tablet, corresponding to the sixth month, which marks the end of the summer season. The two tales may have formed part of a cycle of myths, distributed among the months of the year. The Gilgamesh Epic, however, does not form such a cycle. Both myths have been artificially attached to the adventures of the hero. For the deluge story, we now have the definite proof for its independent existence, through Dr. Poebel's publication of a Sumerian text which embodies the tale, and without any reference to Gilgamesh. Similarly, Scheil and Hilprecht have published fragments of deluge stories written in Akkadian and, likewise, without any connection with the Gilgamesh Epic.

In the Epic, the story leads to another episode attached to Gilgamesh, namely, the search for a magic plant growing in deep water, which has the power of restoring old age to youth. Utanapishtim, the survivor of the deluge, is moved through pity for Gilgamesh, worn out by his long wanderings. At the request of his wife, Utanapishtim decides to tell Gilgamesh of this plant, and the latter succeeds in finding it. He plucks it and decides to take it back to Erech so that all may enjoy the benefit, but, on his way, stops to bathe in a cool cistern. A serpent comes along and snatches the plant from him, and he is forced to return to Erech with his purpose unachieved. Man cannot hope, when old age comes on, to escape death as the end of everything.

Lastly, the twelfth tablet of the Assyrian version of the Gilgamesh Epic is of a purely didactic character, bearing evidence of having been added as a further illustration of the current belief that there is no escape from the nether world to which all must go after life has come to an end. Proper burial and suitable care of the dead represent all that can be done in order to secure a fairly comfortable rest for those who have passed out of this world. Enkidu is once more introduced into this episode. His shade [ghost] is invoked by Gilgamesh and rises up out of the lower world to give a discouraging reply to Gilgamesh's request,

"Tell me, my friend, tell me, my friend,
The law of the earth which thou hast
experienced, tell me."
The mournful message comes back,
"I cannot tell thee, my friend, I cannot tell."

Death is a mystery and must always remain such. The historical Gilgamesh has clearly no connection with the figure introduced into the twelfth tablet. Indeed, as already suggested, the Gilgamesh Epic must have ended with the return to Erech, as related at the close of the eleventh tablet. The twelfth tablet was added by some school-men of Babylonia (or perhaps of Assyria), purely for the purpose of conveying a summary of the teachings in regard to the fate of the dead. Whether these six episodes covering the sixth to the twelfth tablets, (1) the nature myth, (2) the killing of the divine bull, (3) the punishment of Gilgamesh and the death of Enkidu, (4) Gilgamesh's wanderings, (5) the deluge, (6) the search for immortality, were all included at the time that the old Babylonian version was compiled cannot, of course, be determined until we have that version in a more complete form. Since the two tablets thus far recovered show that, as early as 2000 B.C., the Enkidu tale had already been amalgamated with the current stories about Gilgamesh, and the endeavor made to transfer the traits of the former to the latter, it is eminently likely that the story of Ishtar's unhappy love adventure with Gilgamesh was included, as well as Gilgamesh's punishment and the death of Enkidu.

With the evidence furnished by Meissner's fragment of a version of the old Babylonian revision, and by our two tablets, of the early disposition to make popular tales the medium of illustrating current beliefs and the teachings of the temple schools, it may furthermore be concluded that the death of Enkidu and the punishment of Gilgamesh were utilized for didactic purposes in the old Babylonian version. On the other hand, the proof for the existence of the deluge story in the Hammurabi period and some centuries later, independent of any connection with the Gilgamesh Epic, raises the question whether, in the old Babylonian version, of which our two tablets form a part, the deluge tale was already woven into the pattern of the Epic. At all events, till proof to the contrary is forthcoming, we may assume that the twelfth tablet of the Assyrian version, though also reverting to a Babylonian original, dates as the latest addition to the Epic from a period subsequent to 2000 B.C.; and that the same is probably the case with the eleventh tablet.

To sum up, there are four main currents that flow together in the Gilgamesh Epic, even in its old Babylonian form: (1) the adventures of a mighty warrior Enkidu, resting perhaps on a faint tradition of the conquest of Amurru by the hero; (2) the more definite recollection of the exploits of a foreign invader of Babylonia by the name of Gilgamesh, whose home appears likewise to have been in the West; (3) nature myths and didactic tales transferred to Enkidu and Gilgamesh as popular figures; and (4) the process of weaving the traditions, exploits, myths and didactic tales together, in the course of which process Gilgamesh becomes the main hero, and Enkidu his companion.

Furthermore, our investigation has shown that to Enkidu belongs the episode with the woman, used to illustrate the evolution of primitive man to the ways and conditions of civilized life, the conquest of Huwawa in the land of Amurru, the killing of lions and also of the bull, while Gilgamesh is the hero who conquers Erech. Identified with the sun-god, the nature myth of the union of the sun with the earth and the subsequent separation of the two is also transferred to Gilgamesh. The wanderings of the hero, smitten with disease, are a continuation of the nature myth, symbolizing the waning vigor of the sun with the approach of the wintry season.

The details of the process which led to making Gilgamesh the favorite figure, to whom the traits and exploits of Enkidu and of the sun-god are transferred, escape us, but of the fact that Enkidu is the *older* figure, of whom certain adventures were set forth in a tale that once had an independent existence, there can now be little doubt in the face of the evidence furnished by the two ablets of the old Babylonian version; just as the study of these tablets shows that, in the combination of the tales of Enkidu and Gilgamesh, the former is the prototype of which Gilgamesh is the copy. If the two are regarded as brothers, as born in the same place, even resembling one another in appearance and carrying out their adventures in common, it is because, in the process of combination, Gilgamesh becomes the *reflex* of Enkidu. That Enkidu is not the figure created by Aruru to relieve Erech of its tyrannical ruler is also shown by the fact that Gilgamesh remains in control of Erech. It is to Erech that he returns when he fails in his purpose to learn the secret of escape from old age and death. Erech is, therefore, not relieved of the presence of the ruthless ruler through Enkidu. The "Man of Anu," formed by Aruru as a deliver, is confused in the course of the growth of the Epic with Enkidu, the offspring of Ninib, and, in this way, we obtain the strange contradiction of Enkidu and Gilgamesh appearing first as bitter rivals and then as close and inseparable friends. It is of the nature of Epic compositions everywhere to eliminate unnecessary figures by concentrating, on one favorite, the traits belonging to another, or to several others.

The close association of Enkidu and Gilgamesh, which becomes one of the striking features in the combination of the tales of these two heroes, naturally recalls the "Heavenly twins" motif, which has been so fully and so suggestively treated by Professor J. Rendell Harris in his *Cult of the Heavenly Twins*, (London, 1906). Professor Harris has conclusively shown how widespread the tendency is to associate two divine or semi-divine beings in myths and legends as inseparable companions or twins, like Castor and Pollux, Romulus and Remus, the Acvins in the Rig-Veda, Cain and Abel, Jacob and Esau in the Old Testament, the Kabiri of the Phoenicians, Heracles and Iphikles in Greek mythology, Ambrica and Fidelio in Teutonic mythology, Patollo and Potrimpo in old Prussian mythology, Cautes and Cautopates in Mithraism, Jesus and Thomas (according to the Syriac Acts of Thomas), and the various illustrations of "Dioscuri in Christian Legends," set forth by Dr. Harris in his work under this title, which carries the motif far down into the period of legends about Christian Saints who appear in pairs, including the reference to such a pair in Shakespeare's Henry V:

"And Crispin Crispian shall ne'er go by

From that day to the ending of the world." (Act IV, 3, 57-58)

There are, indeed, certain parallels which suggest that Enkidu—Gilgamesh may represent a Babylonian counterpart to the "Heavenly Twins." In the Indo-Iranian, Greek and Roman mythology, the twins almost invariably act together. In unison, they proceed on expeditions to punish enemies.

But, after all, the parallels are of too general a character to be of much moment and, moreover, the parallels stop short at the critical point, for Gilgamesh, though worsted, is not killed by Enkidu, whereas one of the "Heavenly Twins" is always killed by the brother, as Abel is by Cain, and Iphikles by his twin brother Heracles. Even the trait which is frequent in the earliest forms of the "Heavenly Twins," according to which one is immortal and the other is mortal, though applying in a measure to Enkidu, who is killed by Ishtar, while Gilgamesh, the offspring of a divine pair, is only smitten with disease, is too unsubstantial to warrant more than a general comparison between the Enkidu-Gilgamesh pair and the various forms of the "twin" motif found throughout ancient world. For all that, the point is of some interest that in the Gilgamesh Epic we should encounter two figures who are portrayed as possessing the same traits and accomplishing feats in common, which suggests a partial parallel to the various forms in which the twin-motif appears in the mythologies, folk-lore and legends of many nations, and it may be that in some of these instances the duplication is due, as in the case of Enkidu and Gilgamesh, to an actual transfer of the traits of one figure to another who usurped his place.

In concluding this study of the two recently discovered tablets of the old Babylonian version of the Gilgamesh Epic which has brought us several steps further in the interpretation, and in our understanding, of the method of composition of the most notable literary production of ancient Babylonia, it will be proper to consider the *literary* relationship of the old Babylonian to the Assyrian version.

We have already referred to the different form in which the names of the chief figures appear in the old Babylonian version, Gish as against Gish-gi(n)-mash, En-ki-du as against En-ki-doo, Hu-wa-wa as against Hu(m)-ba-ba. Erech appears as *Uruk ribitim,* "Erech of the Plazas," as against *Uruk supuri,* "walled Erech" (or "Erech within the walls"), in the Assyrian version. These variations point to an independent recension for the Assyrian revision; and this conclusion is confirmed by a comparison of parallel passages in our two tablets with the Assyrian version, for such parallels rarely extend to verbal agreements in details and, moreover, show that the Assyrian version has been elaborated.

Beginning with the Pennsylvania tablet, column I is covered in the Assyrian version by tablet I, 5, 25, to 6, 33, though, as pointed out above, in the Assyrian version we have the anticipation of the dreams of Gilgamesh, and their interpretation through their recital to Enkidu by his female companion, whereas in the old Babylonian version we have the dreams *directly* given in a conversation between Gilgamesh and his mother. In the anticipation, there would naturally be some omissions. So lines 4-5 and 12-13 of the Pennsylvania tablet do not appear in the Assyrian version, but in their place is a line (I, 5, 35), to be restored to:

"[I saw him and like] a woman I fell in love with him."

which occurs in the old Babylonian version only in connection with the second dream. The point is of importance as showing that in the Babylonian version the first dream lays stress upon the omen of the falling meteor, as symbolizing the coming of Enkidu, whereas the second dream more specifically reveals Enkidu as a man, of whom Gilgamesh is instantly enamored. Strikingly variant lines, though conveying the same idea, are frequent. Thus, line 14 of the Babylonian version reads:

"I bore it and carried it to thee."

and appears in the Assyrian version (I, 5, 35, supplied from 6, 26),

"I threw it (or him) at thy feet."

with an additional line in elaboration,

"Thou didst bring him into contact with me."

which anticipates the speech of the mother,

(Line 41=Assyrian version I, 6, 33).

Line 10 of the Pennsylvania tablet has *pa-hi-ir* as against *iz-za-az,* I, 5, 31.

Line 8 has *ik-ta-bi-it* as against *da-an* in the Assyrian version I, 5, 29.

More significant is the variant to line 9:

"I became weak and its weight I could not bear."

as against I, 5, 30,

"Its strength was overpowering, and I could not endure its weight."

The important lines 31-36 are not found in the Assyrian version, with the exception of I, 6, 27, which corresponds to lines 33-34, but this lack of correspondence is probably due to the fact that the Assyrian version represents the anticipation of the dreams which, as already suggested, might well omit some details. As against this, we have, in the Assyrian version I, 6, 23-25, an elaboration of line 30 in the Pennsylvania tablet, while, with line 33=line 45 of the Pennsylvania tablet, the parallel between the two versions comes to an end. Lines 34-43 of the Assyrian version (bringing tablet I to a close) represents an elaboration of the speech of Ninsun, followed by a further address of Gilgamesh to his mother, and by the determination of Gilgamesh to seek out Enkidu. Nothing of this sort appears to have been included in the old Babylonian version.

Our text proceeds with the scene between Enkidu and the woman, in which the latter, by her charms and her appeal, endeavors to lead Enkidu away from his life with the animals. From the abrupt manner in which the scene is introduced in line 43 of the Pennsylvania tablet, it is evident that this cannot be the *first* mention of the woman. The meeting must have been recounted in the first tablet, as is the case in the Assyrian version. The second tablet takes up the direct recital of the dreams of Gilgamesh and then continues the narrative. Whether in the old Babylonian version the scene between Enkidu and the woman was described with the same naïve details, as in the Assyrian version, of the sexual intercourse between the two for six days and seven nights cannot, of course, be determined, though presumably the Assyrian version, with the tendency of epics to become more elaborate as they pass from age to age, added some realistic touches. Assuming that lines 44-63 of the Pennsylvania tablet—the cohabitation of Enkidu and the address of the woman—is a repetition of what was already described in the first tablet, the comparison with the Assyrian version I, 4, 16-41, not only points to the elaboration of the later version, but likewise to an independent recension, even where parallel lines can be picked out. Only lines 46-48 of the Pennsylvania tablet form a complete parallel to line 21 of column 4 of the Assyrian version. The description in lines 22-32 of column 4 is missing, though it may, of course, have been included, in part, in the recital in the first tablet of the old Babylonian version. Lines 49-59 of the Pennsylvania tablet are covered by 33-39, the only slight difference being the specific mention in line 58 of the Pennsylvania tablet of Eanna, the temple in Erech, described as "the dwelling of Anu," whereas, in the Assyrian version, Eanna is merely referred to as the "holy house" and described as "the dwelling of Anu and Ishtar," where Ishtar is clearly a later addition.

Leaving aside lines 60-61, which may be merely a variant (though independent) of line 39 of column 4 of the Assyrian version, we now have in the Pennsylvania tablet a second speech of the woman to Enkidu (not represented in the Assyrian version) beginning, like the first one, with *alka*, "Come" (lines 62-63), in which she asks Enkidu to leave the "accursed ground" in which he dwells. This speech, as the description which follows, extending into columns 3-4, and telling how the woman clothed Enkidu, how she brought him to the sheepfolds, how she taught him to eat bread and to drink wine, and how she instructed him in the ways of civilization, must have been included in the second tablet of the Assyrian version which has come down to us in a very imperfect form. Nor is the scene in which Enkidu and Gilgamesh have their encounter found in the preserved portions of the second (or possibly the third) tablet of the Assyrian version, but only a brief reference to it in the fourth tablet, in which, in Epic style, the story is repeated, leading up to the second exploit—the joint campaign of Enkidu and Gilgamesh against Huwawa. This reference, covering only seven lines, corresponds to lines 192-231 of the Pennsylvania tablet; but, the former being the repetition and the latter the original recital, the comparison to be instituted merely reveals again the independence of the Assyrian version, as shown in the use of *kibsu*, "tread" (IV, 2, 46), for *sepu*, "foot" (line 216), *i-na-us*, "quake" (line 5C), as against *ir-tu-tu* (lines 221 and 226).

Such variants as,
Gish eribam ul iddin (line 217)
against
Gilgamesh ana surubi ul namdin (IV, 2, 47)
and again,

issabtuma kima lim "they grappled at the gate of the family house" (IV, 2,
48),

against

issaabtuma ina bab bit emuti, "they grappled at the gate of the family house"
IV, 2, 48),

ll point once more to the literary independence of the Assyrian version. The end
of the conflict and the reconciliation of the two heroes is likewise missing in the
Assyrian version. It may have been referred to at the beginning of column 3 of
ablet IV.

Coming to the Yale tablet, the few passages in which a comparison may be
nstituted with the fourth tablet of the Assyrian version, to which, in a general way,
t must correspond, are not sufficient to warrant any conclusions, beyond the
confirmation of the literary independence of the Assyrian version. The section
comprised within lines 72-89, where Enkidu's grief at his friend's decision to fight
Huwawa is described, and he makes confession of his own physical exhaustion,
may correspond to tablet IV, column 4, of the Assyrian version. This would fit in
with the beginning of the reverse, the first two lines of which (136-137) correspond
o column 5 of the fourth tablet of the Assyrian version, with a variation "seven-
fold fear," as against "fear of men" in the Assyrian version. If lines 138-139 (in
column 4) of the Yale tablet correspond to line 7 of column 5 of tablet IV of the
Assyrian version, we would again have an illustration of the elaboration of the later
version by the addition of lines 3-6. But beyond this we have merely the
comparison of the description of Huwawa:

"Whose roar is a flood, whose mouth is fire, and whose breath is death,"
which occurs twice in the Yale tablet (lines 110-111 and 196-197), with the same
phrase in the Assyrian version tablet IV, 5, 3—but here, as just pointed out, with an
elaboration. Practically, therefore, the entire Yale tablet represents an addition to
our knowledge of the Huwawa episode, and, until we are fortunate enough to
discover more fragments of the fourth tablet of the Assyrian version, we must
content ourselves with the conclusions reached from a comparison of the
Pennsylvania tablet with the parallels in the Assyrian version.

It may be noted, as a general point of resemblance in the exterior form of the
old Babylonian and Assyrian versions, that both were inscribed on tablets
containing six columns, three on the obverse and three on the reverse; and that the
length of the tablets—an average of 40 to 50 lines—was about the same, thus
revealing, in the external form, a conventional size for the tablets in the older
period, which was carried over into later times.

New Haven
1920

The End

...

Gilgamesh

Gilgamesh

Gilgamesh

Gilgamesh

Gilgamesh

Gilgamesh

Made in the USA
Middletown, DE
08 August 2015